"I've got three k
real estate busin

An inscrutable emotion flickered in Tom's amber eyes. "No woman worth her salt would want to play second fiddle to all that."

Aware she was beginning to want to kiss him, Emma busied herself wiping down counters. "Mmm. I don't know." Tamping down her unwanted desire, she sent him a teasing look over her shoulder. "You might be selling yourself short."

Grooves deepened on either side of his mouth. "What do you mean?" he asked in the low, flirtatious tone she loved.

Aware how easy it would be to fall for this sexy cowboy all over again, Emma ticked off his attributes with all the passion of a grocery list, read aloud. "Three adorable kids. A mom who lives in and loves to help out."

"That's all?"

With effort, she forced herself to meet his probing gaze. Aware the air between them was quickly becoming way too intimate and highly charged, she shrugged, adding, "Financial security."

He leaned in close, mimicking her low tone perfectly. "Nothing else going for me?"

She swallowed around the sudden parched feeling in her throat. Aware that if she wanted to, she could come up with a heck of a lot more.

Dear Reader,

People dream big in Texas. The bigger and brasher the goal, the better. This is the case for Emma Lockhart and Tom Reid. United from childhood, they dated all through high school and college, and even planned to marry. *After* they finished business school at a prestigious Ivy League college.

Unfortunately, life happens when you are busy making other plans. Tragedy struck. Tom could no longer hold up his end of the bargain. Emma sympathized with her fiancé's plight, but not to the point where she was willing to summarily give up all their mutual ambitions. Whereas Tom wanted *new dreams*. Unable to broker a solution, they went their separate ways.

Six and a half years later, Emma is back in Laramie County. Big degree and sought-after apprenticeship under her belt, she is no closer to fame and fortune than when she left. Tom, meanwhile, is living the dream. Sadly, he is a widower now, but he has three adorable four-and-a-half-year-old sons. As well as two thriving businesses, the family ranch and commercial real estate.

For months, they are able to avoid each other, but when Tom becomes Emma's landlord and is tasked with possibly helping her achieve the pursuit that drove her out of his arms, he has a decision to make. As does she. Because she has fallen in love with his triplet sons, and they want her to be their mommy. What is a woman to do when she knows she can't have it all? Or can she...?

I hope you enjoy this story as much as I loved writing it.

Best wishes,

Cathy Gillen Thacker

The Triplets' Secret Wish

CATHY GILLEN THACKER

HARLEQUIN
SPECIAL
EDITION

ISBN-13: 978-1-335-40859-4

The Triplets' Secret Wish

Copyright © 2022 by Cathy Gillen Thacker

For questions and comments about the quality of this book, please contact us at CustomerService@Harlequin.com.

Harlequin Enterprises ULC
22 Adelaide St. West, 41st Floor
Toronto, Ontario M5H 4E3, Canada
www.Harlequin.com

Printed in U.S.A.

Cathy Gillen Thacker is a married mother of three. She and her husband reside in North Carolina. Her stories have made numerous appearances on bestseller lists, but her best reward is knowing one of her books made someone's day a little brighter. A popular Harlequin author, she loves telling passionate stories with happy endings and thinks nothing beats a good romance and a hot cup of tea! Visit her at cathygillenthacker.com for information on her books, recipes and a list of her favorite things.

Books by Cathy Gillen Thacker

Harlequin Special Edition

Lockharts Lost & Found

His Plan for the Quadruplets
Four Christmas Matchmakers
The Twin Proposal
Their Texas Triplets
Their Texas Christmas Gift

Texas Legends: The McCabes

The Texas Cowboy's Quadruplets
His Baby Bargain
Their Inherited Triplets

Harlequin Western Romance

Texas Legends: The McCabes

The Texas Cowboy's Triplets
The Texas Cowboy's Baby Rescue

Visit the Author Profile page
at Harlequin.com for more titles.

Chapter One

"*You're* the landlord?" Her heart pounding, Emma Lockhart stared at Tom Reid in astonishment, taking in his ruggedly handsome face and tall, broad-shouldered frame. Over six years had passed since they had abruptly ended their engagement. Yet here he was. Still heartache personified.

Tom paused next to the historic brick commercial building on the Laramie, Texas, street, as powerfully commanding as ever in that uniquely Texas cowboy way. The corners of his lips curving upward, he tipped the brim of his Stetson at her. "ABC Properties at your service, ma'am."

The familiarity of his gaze rankled almost as much as his irresistible physical presence. Emma folded her arms in front of her, forcing herself to ignore the way his tan shirt and dark jeans molded to his muscular body. "First of all—" she drew a deep breath, pushing aside the scorching hot memories of the two of them making love "—don't call me, ma'am!"

And stop looking at me like you want to kiss me again, ASAP!

His golden brown eyes twinkled mischievously. "What would you prefer I call you?" he taunted. He leaned toward her, the ends of his sable brown hair and his smooth, suntanned skin catching the dazzling April sunlight. "Princess Lady Emma?"

Her dreaded childhood nickname. Coined by the sexy mischief-maker in front of her, no less. Pretending a cool she couldn't begin to feel, Emma squared her shoulders. "Miss Lockhart would be fine."

He lifted a brow at her arch tone. Using humor and outrageous behavior the way he always did, to keep others at arm's length, emotionally. "Going formal?" he drawled.

A pleasurable warmth baked down from the sun overhead, and there was nary a cloud in the deep blue Texas sky. She kept her eyes locked on his. "Might be wise," she retorted. "Given how things stand between us."

His smile faded. For a moment, he looked like the grieving widowed dad of four-year-old triplets, who, after two long years, was still working hard to get his life all the way back on track. "And how is that?"

His silky smooth voice ratcheted up the tension inside her even more. "Awkward. Tense."

A provoking grin tugged at the corners of his lips once again. "You mean unforgiving?"

A torrent of longing, destined to go unmet, welled up within her. Reminding herself how quickly he had moved on after their breakup, marrying and starting a family within a year, while she had struggled on alone, Emma frowned. "I forgave you a long time ago."

She'd had no choice but to do so.

Tom squinted. He ran the flat of his palm beneath his jaw, stroking thoughtfully. "Which is funny," he drawled. "Because—" he aimed a thumb at the center of his chest "—I don't think I ever did anything wrong."

She turned her glance away from all that hard male muscle, and conjured up the heartache from years past to help keep him at arm's length. "You reneged on our plans to go to Wharton together, to get our MBAs."

Sorrow tautened his handsome face. Ah, yes. The loss of his wife wasn't the only tragedy he had suffered in the last decade. "My dad died, Emma. I had to stay here to take care of the ranch."

She remembered the anguish of losing Samuel Reid. She had been close to him, too. "I'm not debating that." Her voice grew as rusty as Tom's. Their last semester at Texas Tech had been horrendous in the aftermath of his father's death. "But you could have joined me after you got things set up at the Rocking R ranch."

He stood, legs braced apart, arms folded in front of him. "I couldn't leave my mom."

Ignoring the hurt that had dogged her for months afterward, Emma balled her fists at her sides and blurted out angrily, "Your mom encouraged you to go on with your plans." And in fact, had been really disappointed in Tom when he hadn't.

Another long pause as he regarded her with those mesmerizing eyes. "My dad's fatal heart attack devastated her," he reminded Emma curtly. "It wouldn't have been right to leave."

There, they disagreed. Always had. Always would, probably. He knew it, too.

He returned to the matter at hand. "Do you want to see the space?"

"Yes." Emma forced herself to regard him with the same businesslike cool he was using with her. "If you wouldn't mind."

Like all the historic downtown buildings, the two-story unit on Main Street was made of brick and featured a fancy beveled glass door and beautiful plate-glass windows. The floors inside were gleaming oak. The thousand-square-foot first floor was divided into three spaces. A large area at the front, where the retail space could be. Another slightly smaller space just behind it, where she would be able to situate her design studio. The third area contained a small break room, a restroom and a storage area, as well as a service door that opened up on the alley. Pointing to a staircase, he explained that it led to a second floor apartment.

Acutely aware of his nearness, Emma cleared her throat and asked, "Why did the former tenant leave?" It didn't really matter, since the business/retail space was so desirable. She just needed to make conversation so she could stop focusing on him. And how emotional he always made her feel. There were no dull days with Tom Reid. She was happy or sad. Angry or entranced. And always completely overwhelmed. "He needed more room, so he moved his insurance agency to the big new business center on the outskirts of town."

"Ah...makes sense." Noticing a bottle of hand soap was a little too close to the edge of the break room counter, Emma moved to set it back before it fell. Tom reached in to rescue it, too, his tall, strong body briefly brushing hers. Her heart began to pound. "How long have you owned this place?" she asked, moving back out into the front rooms.

He followed. "Almost six years."

Curious, she turned to face him. "So you bought it...?"

"Yeah, the year after my dad died, with some of the life insurance money. I wanted to make sure my mom was taken care of, and I was more comfortable putting the money into property here than commodities or the stock market."

Emma nodded, knowing for the risk-averse like him, that certainly made sense. She studied the walls, which were a soft pearl gray, and appreciated that they would provide a sophisticated neutral background. "This looks recently painted," she noted in admiration.

"The first floor has been."

"And the second?" she asked.

He shrugged. "I was going to let the tenant decide on colors."

"But there is a painting allowance?"

"Yes."

Not wanting to stand too close to him, Emma paced the width of the casually elegant space. "What about other changes?"

He remained where he was, standing straight and tall. "I don't want to do anything structural," he told her. "That would be a permit nightmare. But small cosmetic updates are permissible within reason." He studied her a long moment before finally moving nearer. "What are you thinking?" His brow furrowed. "A small shoe or boot store?"

Emma envisioned out loud. "A design studio and sales boutique, actually."

He nodded, still regarding her intently, reminding her how much his support had once meant to her.

Ignoring the catch in her throat, she went on, "I want a place to showcase my footwear. I think that will be easier if I have a professional space in town, rather than just a workroom at my parents' ranch."

"Makes sense…"

Disappointment swirled through her. She felt the "but" coming on.

"You think there is that much of a market for expensive shoes in Laramie County? Other than the hand-tooled western boots they already make at Monroe's Western Wear?"

Leave it to him to immediately point out the purported flaw in her strategy. "Obviously, I am looking to expand my business."

He charmed her with a smile. "To…?"

"Other cities. Like Dallas and Houston and Austin. And maybe beyond that, too."

He regarded her with new respect. "How long do you think that will take?"

"Six months, hopefully."

Intuitive amber eyes lassoed hers. He swept off his hat, and ran his fingers through the rumpled strands of his dark brown hair. "And then what? Will you keep the store here as your flagship shop?" He settled his black Stetson back on his head.

"Probably not."

He frowned. "So you're asking for what then?" he countered skeptically. "A six month lease?"

That was all the money she had socked away. The rest was being spent on materials and promotion for this next phase of her fledgling business. Barely able to look at him and not wonder what it would be like to kiss him again, she nodded her confirmation. "Yes."

"Then we have a problem," he told her.

Tom Reid wasn't surprised to see irritation turn the corners of Emma's luscious lips down. She had never liked being told no. To anything.

Nor had he ever liked disappointing her.

But business was business, as she had once schooled him roundly. He stepped forward, purposefully invading her space.

Her pretty face flushed with indignant color. At five foot seven inches, she was still curvy in all the right places. Her peachy skin was flawless, her slender nose straight and perfect, her expressive eyes a deep emerald. Emma's chestnut locks fell to her shoulders in soft, silken waves, which he had always found enormously sexy. And she had a lush lower lip, just right for kissing.

Not that they would ever likely be doing that again...

If he ever found himself getting serious about a woman again—and frankly, he couldn't really see himself doing that, given how complicated and busy his life was—then it would be with a woman who wanted all the same things he did. Marriage. Family. A home here on his family ranch in Laramie County...

That was not, had never been, Emma.

As the silence lengthened, he let his gaze drift over her floral knit dress, with the cap sleeves, formfitting bodice and swirling skirt that ended just above her knees.

Lower still, she wore sexy ankle boots, with a spike heel that showed off her spectacularly shapely legs.

Pushing away the desire pulsing inside him, he told her matter-of-factly, "The standard lease here for commercial property is three to five years. And most prefer five."

A quirk of her elegant brows. When she spoke, her voice was soft, persuasive. "Can't you make an exception?"

Could he?

To give himself time to decide, he gestured at the stairs. "You haven't seen the second-floor apartment yet."

Emma paused, her slender hand gripping the wood railing. "You say that like there's a problem."

Actually, there was. And it had nothing to do with his sudden, reckless desire to flirt with her. Test the waters, just a little bit. Cryptically, he admitted, "There are what some might consider issues." Especially if they were women who were used to the finer things in life.

She moved to give him room and indicated he should go first. "Lead the way then."

He climbed the stairs. By the time he had unlocked and opened the door, she was standing beside him.

The dismay he expected never came. She looked at the tall windows that faced Main Street, as if already envisioning living happily there. Then she whirled back to him, her enthusiasm building. "I love the high ceilings. They make it feel really spacious. The light is spectacular, too."

Surprised at how good it felt to have her close again, even for something as mundane as this, he pointed to the other side of the front room.

Although the wood floors throughout were in fine shape, there were other problems that still needed to be addressed before anyone moved into the apartment.

"The stove and refrigerator both need to be replaced," he told her. "Same with the faucet on the kitchen sink."

"Do they work now?"

"Yes, but there is no telling for how long. Plus…" He pointed at the miniscule number of cabinets. "There is no dishwasher or disposal. And I'm not sure the plumbing will support putting either in."

"That's okay. I've made do with just a microwave, mini-fridge and a sink before."

He remembered.

When they'd been in college, they'd made many a date night supper together in their dorm rooms. And always made love afterward...

Not that he needed to be remembering that.

"So, for me, even the most basic apartment kitchen seems like heaven." She shrugged, as if not caught up in similar memories. "Besides, there are plenty of good restaurants and shops within walking distance."

"True." But how long before that, too, would get old? Have her wanting to move on? *Again?*

He had already lost her once.

Then his wife, to a hellacious illness.

He had no interest in going through heartbreak a third time, and whether he liked it or not, any dalliance with Emma was likely to eventually lead to just that. Unless, of course, they kept their emotions out of it. Made it strictly casual. Then....

She gave him a coolly assessing look and shook her head. Heading into the adjacent bedroom, whose ecru paint was as dingy as the rest of the living space, she paused to check out the arched windows that overlooked the county's premiere shopping district. "I don't know why you would think I am so fussy."

Her dig hit the target. Not afraid to go toe-to-toe with her, he lobbed one right back. "You are the one who wanted to be rich and famous."

It was her turn to be taken aback. Something flickered in her eyes, then disappeared, and the corners of her delectable lips curled downward. "Well, as we both know," she said with a beleaguered sigh, "that hasn't happened yet."

But she still wanted it to; that was clear.

And that meant there was no future for the two of them. Not with he and his three boys making their home in rural west Texas.

Forcing himself to get back to the business of showing the residence, he showed her the bathroom, which was as out-of-date as the rest of the property. The floor was black linoleum, the old nondescript fixtures, including the shower stall, a standard white. It, too, needed to be repainted. "This all could be redone, if you are willing to fold the upgrade cost into the price of the lease and wait for the work to be complete."

She waved an airy hand. "That's not necessary."

Which was exactly what his last tenant, a surgical resident at the hospital, had said. "Planning to rough it?"

"Focus on what is important," she corrected him.

A taut silence fell between them. "Your work," he said finally, not sure why he found that so disappointing. After all, it wasn't any of his business. They both had their own lives now.

She nodded in acknowledgment. "Yes." Their eyes locked. Held. Without warning, he wondered how it would feel to be close to her again.

Oblivious to the nature of his thoughts, she raked her teeth across her lower lip. "If I give you the security deposit and first and last month's rent today, could I move in this weekend?" she asked.

"What's the rush? Your folks throwing you off their ranch?" Where she had been living for the last year and a half.

She made a face, as if that were the dumbest thing she had ever heard. "No. Of course not."

"Then the answer is no."

Her chin took on the stubborn tilt he knew so well. "Why not?" she demanded, as if he were the one being unreasonable.

"Because I want all the work done to both our satisfaction before you sign the lease and move in."

Huffing out a breath, she folded her arms in front of her, tightening the fabric of her dress across the soft, rounded curves of her breasts. "How long will that take?"

Aware it was taking everything he had not to haul her into his arms and kiss her, if only to see if they still had the same explosive chemistry as before, he calculated. "We're probably looking at early June."

She stared at him, aghast. "*Five weeks!* Are you serious?"

Funny, he didn't recall her ever being this demanding. Or unreasonable.

"It takes time to schedule a painting crew, especially this time of year, when everyone wants to get work done, and the materials are on special order. The appliances are supposed to come in the end of May. The kitchen faucet in about two weeks or so."

She closed her eyes and rubbed her temples, as if she had a giant headache coming on. "Can't we just deal with all that later?"

"It'll be a lot more of a hassle after you move in."

"So?" She propped her hands on her curvaceous hips. Beginning to look more than a little piqued, she prodded, "If I don't care, why should you?"

He moved closer, curious about what she was holding back. For reasons he did not want to examine too closely, her refusal to fully confide in him, irked the heck out of him.

Maybe because they had been down this road before?

He took in the pink color staining her cheeks, and the exasperated twist of her full, soft lips. His body hardening in response, he countered gruffly, "Give me a reason why we need to do this only on your terms."

"And maybe you'll be more amenable?" she queried.

"Exactly."

Her eyes narrowed. "And if I don't?"

He shrugged, beginning to wonder if it would be worth the trouble to have her as a tenant. They'd only spent twenty minutes together, and he was already frustrated as hell with her. "Then it will be business as usual. And you can take possession of both spaces, simultaneously, when they are completely ready, in five or six weeks."

Emma knew that time frame would not work for her. She also knew unless she confided something to Tom, that he would not relent on what would be, in any other situation, a reasonable business decision on his part. Which left her only one choice, to open up to him again, just a little bit.

"The reason for the rush is that I have to get my design studio and work space operational well before the next two weeks are up."

His amber eyes sparkled the way they always did when he got under her skin. He leaned in close. Stared her right in the eye. "Because…?"

Damn, he was nosy and difficult. "You promise you won't tell anyone?"

"Cross my heart."

Emma fought back a reaction to all that testosterone. "I've got someone coming here to meet with me about acquiring one of my footwear designs."

"One?"

She jerked in a bolstering breath and returned his smile. "I know it doesn't sound like it but it's a big deal."

Another quirk of his dark brow. "Then why don't you want anyone to know?"

Trying not to think what his steady appraisal and deep voice did to her, Emma cleared her throat. "Because I've spoken too soon before."

Realization lit his eyes. "When you first got back to Texas, and thought you had a deal with that ritzy bridal salon in Houston."

She blinked, surprised he had kept up with what was going on in her life, post breakup. "You know about that, too?"

"Everyone in town did. They all thought you were

going to be the queen of the thousand-dollar wedding boot."

"But not you?" she prodded.

He thought a moment. Then said with what appeared to be sincere honesty, "I hoped it would work out for you."

"But it didn't," Emma said in discouragement. "And for months I went around answering questions about what had gone wrong and accepting condolences." She sighed again.

Tom continued studying her. "Is that why you went back to Italy recently? Were you thinking about working there again?"

Still leery of revealing too much, she admitted cautiously, "I thought it would help me figure things out if I went back to Le Marche and visited the family shoe company, where I did my apprenticeship."

"And did it?"

Sadly, yes. But not about to tell Tom or anyone else about that gargantuan misunderstanding and heartbreak, for fear of bringing on even more embarrassment to herself, and/or pity from others, she simply said, "Yeah, it did."

The trip had helped her realize she was going to have to be even more aggressive if she ever wanted to fully realize her ambition.

So, she had come back to Texas, ready to work her heart out again, only to be on the receiving end of a serendipitous miracle and have a contact she had been pursuing for nearly two years reach out to her. With *real* interest this time.

Which was why she had to get this space! "So, are you going to help me out here or not?"

Before he could answer her, his phone buzzed. "Sorry." He pulled it out of his pocket. "With kids, you can never not check to see who is calling or texting..."

As he scanned the screen, his expression tautened in a way that let her know something was wrong. Her pulse quickened in alarm. "What is it?"

Tom's face was ashen. "My mom is at the grocery store with the triplets. Apparently, she hit her head and may need stitches. I'm going to have to go."

"I'll come with you."

He gave her a look.

"I love Marjorie," Emma said fiercely. *Always had, always would.* "And from the sound of it, you're going to need help."

His hesitation faded. "All right. But I don't want to waste time. So, you ride with me."

Chapter Two

Emma hadn't ridden with Tom since the night they had broken up. The Silverado pickup truck he was driving now was a lot more luxurious than the basic model he'd had back then, yet sitting in the passenger seat beside him, still felt oddly right. As if she—and everyone in his orbit—were protected by his steady masculine presence. She had missed that feeling, more than she had realized.

Fortunately, he was focused on the morning traffic in the heart of Laramie, and the town's big, new supermarket was not far away. And did not pick up on her unprecedented sentimentality.

The store manager, Lydia Cabot, was waiting for them at the front door.

"Where's my mom?" Tom asked anxiously.

Lydia pointed to the produce section, where a small crowd had gathered. They rushed over. Seeing the big, tall rancher approaching, people moved aside to let him pass, while Emma held back, careful to give them the room they needed.

"Mom!" Tom knelt beside Marjorie. One of his four-year-old triplet sons was sitting next to his youthful-looking grandmother. His face was pale, but he was outwardly calm. The other two were nowhere in sight. Tom gestured at the gauze Marjorie was holding pressed to her hairline, just above her left temple, the spill of blood down her yoga clothes. "What happened?"

"It was silly, really." His mom flushed in embarrassment. "I bent down to get something and caught the corner of the apple bin on my way back up."

Meg Carrigan, the nursing supervisor at the local hospital, eased back toward them, first aid kit in hand. From the way she was dressed, Emma surmised she had been shopping, too. Meg looked at Marjorie, then Tom. "I called the urgent care. They said they can take her if she comes over now."

"Okay. We'll get her there." Tom looked around. Then back at the child sitting next to Marjorie, his small body pressed close to hers. "Where are Bowie and Crockett? Austin, where are your brothers?"

The little boy hedged.

"Out with it," Tom demanded.

Austin wrinkled his nose. "They didn't want to get in trouble."

Uh-oh, Emma thought, sensing trouble ahead.

Tom's brow furrowed. "Why would they...? Never mind. We'll talk about that later. Where did they go?"

"They might be hiding," Austin conceded reluctantly. "I'll go get them."

Tom looked from his son to his mom, torn.

"I'll go with Austin," Emma volunteered.

He met her eyes, the angst between them earlier gone. "Thanks." He looked at his son. "Listen to Miss Emma, Austin."

"Yes, Daddy."

Austin scurried off, with Emma right behind him.

She noted he seemed to be making a beeline for the far end of the store. "I guess you know where they are?"

His slender shoulders lifted in a hapless shrug. "They like to hide where we build forts when Grandma is busy talking to one of her friends."

He reached aisle number 12. Laundry detergents and other soaps lined the right side. The left was filled with paper products. On the lower shelf, several big packages of paper towels seemed to be listing off the edge. They were moving, too. "Bowie and Crockett!" Austin yelled at the two small figures crouched behind them. "You got to come out now!"

Two little heads popped up over the edge of the packages. They were identical to their triplet brother and cute as could be. Although all three seemed to be sporting different haircuts. Emma guessed as a way to help tell them apart.

"Daddy is here," Austin continued, looking like a miniature grown-up with his short, layered haircut.

"Who are you?" the one with the Prince Valiant hairstyle asked suspiciously.

"I am Miss Emma. One of your daddy's and grand-mother's family friends." Belatedly, she realized how difficult it must be for Tom to handle this rambunc-tious trio without his late wife there to help him raise them. Although his mother lived with them and was very involved. "And who are you?" She knelt and held out her hand.

He reached over the barrier and took it reluctantly, giving a short, confident shake. "Crockett."

"And you are…?" she asked the final boy with the short, rumpled haircut that looked like it never saw a brush.

"Bowie."

She shook his hand, too. Surprised at how strong and purposeful his grip was as well.

Tom must have taught his boys the proper way to shake hands. Not to be outdone, Austin shook her hand, too. She smiled. "Well, it's a pleasure to meet all three of you."

Already back on task, Austin stomped his little boot-clad foot. "You have to come with me to see Daddy!" he repeated to his brothers.

Loud sighs followed. The plastic wall of packages crinkled, but they made no move to come out into the aisle.

"Is he mad at us?" Crockett asked worriedly.

Imagining they'd had quite a scare, and hence had every reason to run away, Emma moved the packages and cleared an exit for Crockett and Bowie. Still hunkered down to face them, she kept her demeanor as kind and gentle as possible. "Why would he be upset with you?"

"'Cause it was our fault Gramma got hurt," Bowie said with a grimace.

Crockett agreed. "We were throwing apples at each other."

"They were yelling," Austin added matter-of-factly, "and they made a big mess."

"What were you doing when all this was going on?" Emma asked him.

"I was getting clementine oranges for my school lunch," Austin admitted.

"Is Gramma gonna be okay?" Crockett asked.

Emma guided them both off their perches. "It appears that way, but I think we should go see her and find out just to be sure. In any case, you can say you're sorry."

"Okay."

All three boys fell into step beside her.

By the time they reached the produce section, Marjorie was seated in a folding chair, a clean bandage wrapped around her forehead. She was still a little pale, but otherwise seemed completely calm and composed. Tom was standing beside her, brawny arms folded in front of him. His handsome face was etched with worry. "Mom, you have to let me take you to the doctor."

Rather than answering him, she smiled at her three grandsons as they approached to stand contritely in front of her.

"We're sorry, Gramma. We didn't mean to misbe-have," Crockett said, apologizing sincerely.

"Or make you bump your head," Bowie added.

"Or argue about what fruit to get," Austin said, his lower lip trembling with anxiety. "Are you really gonna be okay?"

"Yes, I am." Marjorie smiled. She hugged each of her grandchildren in turn. "It was just a little accident. You-all don't need to worry about it."

The triplets sighed their relief, but still looked a little guilty.

It was clear from the disappointed and exasper-ated expression on Tom's face that even if their grand-mother had given the boys a pass, he hadn't. And would be having a talk with them. Just not here, and not now. Not when there were more urgent matters to tend to…

Marjorie turned her attention back to her son. "You can drop me off at the urgent care clinic, if you in-sist, but then the boys have to go to pre-K. They are late already."

"I could go with you, Marjorie," Emma volunteered. "If you'd be all right with me driving your minivan, that is."

"Actually, that would be great," the older woman said with a relieved smile.

Tom looked at Emma. "You sure?" he asked, his voice a low, sexy rumble. "I'll get there as soon as I can, but since they are late, I have to go through the whole sign-in process and then walk them to their classroom." Which meant it could take a while.

She told herself she was doing this for his mother, not for him. "It's no problem," she replied. "I would be happy to help."

Emma sat in the waiting room, while Marjorie went back to an exam room to get stitched up. Twenty minutes in, she got a text from Tom.

Mom doing okay?

Far as I know. Boys get checked in to school?

Yes, but the school director wants to talk to me. Can I have the meeting now, or should I reschedule?

Do it now. I'll drive your mom home, if she finishes before you get here.

Thanks, Emma. Appreciate it.

Her insides warmed as she read his message. Funny. They had managed not to talk in the years since they had broken up, yet today, it almost felt as if hardly any time had elapsed.

Why was that?

She had no chance to ponder it.

Marjorie came out, her forehead bandaged neatly. "That was fast." Emma rose.

"I only needed four stitches."

"Well, that's good." Emma fell into step beside her, then held the glass door open, letting Marjorie go through first. "Tom was delayed at the school. He said the director wanted to meet with him. So, I'm going to drive you home, if that is okay with you."

"Sounds perfect."

They caught up a little, while Emma drove out to the Rocking R ranch. The nicely cultivated spread had been in the Reid family for generations. A stream cut through the center of the property, and Wagyu cattle took the place of the Black Angus his dad used to raise. As they drew nearer, Emma saw a small bunkhouse now sat behind the barns and stable. The rambling two story cedar-and-stone ranch house was just the way she recalled it, save what looked to be a tall privacy fence that closed in the backyard and a big wooden play fort/swing set.

"Is it my imagination or is the Rocking R larger than it used to be?"

Marjorie shook her head. "Still the same ten thousand acres." She gazed around with pride. "Tom would like to acquire more land, to build up the business, but nothing is for sale right now. Which is why he went in to commercial property."

How come she hadn't known that? Oh, yeah. Probably because when anyone brought up his name to her, which wasn't often, she cut them off and changed the subject. Now, though, she found herself wanting to know what was going on with him. "He's successful then?"

Marjorie beamed. "Oh, yes. Very. Which isn't surprising because all he does is work and care for his family."

Emma could believe that.

"Would you like to come in for a few minutes?"

Emma figured she should make sure Marjorie was settled before she left. "I'd love to, thanks." She circled around to get her door for her, noting Tom's mom seemed drained from the events of the morning.

Marjorie shifted her bag over her shoulder. Her petite form was several inches shorter than Emma's own, although probably thanks to the yoga classes she took, she was slim and fit as ever. "How about a cappuccino?" she asked.

Emma's mouth watered at the thought. "Sounds perfect."

The older woman led the way into the ranch house and down the familiar hallway to the large country kitchen at the rear. Emma gestured at the party hats and colorful noisemakers strewn across the big round table in the center of the room. A gift box stood open at the place where Marjorie had always sat when Emma visited the house years ago. "What is all this?"

"An early birthday and Mother's Day gift from Tom and the boys." Marjorie plucked a glossy brochure from the tissue paper and handed it over.

Emma stared in wonderment. "A two-week eating tour of Italy! Complete with cooking lessons from some of the country's best chefs. Wow…you're finally going to get to go!"

"I wish." Marjorie stood in front of a deluxe espresso maker with all the bells and whistles, her shoulders slumped with what appeared to be escalating fatigue.

Realizing what a morning she must have had, Emma gently guided her toward a chair. "How about I fix our beverages," she said.

"You know how to use it? I upgraded to a new model recently and it's a bit complicated."

"No worries... I got this. I worked my way through college and business school as a barista, remember?"

"True." Marjorie sat back with a sigh and a smile.

"One cappuccino coming right up!" Aware being here with Tom's mom felt just as comfortable as being with him in his truck, Emma went about making the espresso and putting the milk on to steam and froth before turning back to her host. "So, tell me about this trip," she said as the machine began to work its magic. "When are you supposed to leave?"

"On Saturday."

She got out two cups and saucers. "That's three days from now!"

"Yes." Marjorie lifted a desultory hand. "But obviously, I can't go."

"Because of the stitches?"

She shook her head. "No. Those will self-dissolve when the waterproof seal they put over them, peels off a week from now."

"Then?"

"Tom can't handle his boys on his own!"

Emma lounged against the counter, as the aromatic fragrance of freshly brewed espresso and steamed milk filled the room. "Obviously, he thinks he can, or he wouldn't have gotten you such a wonderful gift."

Marjorie pinched the bridge of her nose. "You saw the chaos at the grocery store this morning."

"Are the boys always like that?"

"Whenever they get worked up or worried about something, yes, they are."

"And right now, they're worried about…?"

"Me, not being here." Marjorie sighed.

A thoughtful silence fell.

"Can't you and Tom get a part-time sitter?" Emma asked.

"Maybe, if we had more time. But we don't. So, I'm just going to have to call Edith, Cynthia and Sally, and let them know I can't go."

Emma blinked. "Your three best friends are going with you?"

"Yes." Marjorie ran a hand through her short silver-blond hair. "It was part of the surprise."

Emma sprinkled a little cinnamon on the top of the cappuccino and set the older woman's drink in front of her. "Then you have to go, Marjorie."

She remained unconvinced.

Emma put a latte on for herself, then turned back, determined to talk sense into Tom's mom. "For so many years you have given so much of yourself, and sacrificed everything you wanted to do, in order to care for your loved ones. For once, you need to think about yourself."

"I agree," a gruff male voice said from the doorway.

They looked up to see Tom standing there. Neither of them had heard him come in. He hung his hat on a hook near the back door and ran his hands through his dark hair, restoring order to the rumpled strands. The corners of his mouth took on a downward slant. "Rest assured, the boys know what they did was wrong today," he told his mom. "They promised me they won't act up like that in the grocery store again."

Marjorie did not seem worried about that. "What did the preschool director want to talk to you about?"

Tom exhaled, for a moment looking more overwhelmed than Emma had ever seen him. "She wants me to think about putting them in separate classes."

Marjorie's eyes widened. "In the middle of the school year?"

"Yeah, but they indicated that they would be switching a lot of kids around at the same time. They think it would help the kids handle change."

Marjorie frowned. "Or foster separation anxiety."

"They all have recess at the same time, so they would be able to see each other then."

Marjorie considered this. She looked at her son, the affection palpable between them. "What did you tell the director?"

He offered a curt smile. "Yes."

"When would they do this?" his mom pressed.

"Next week."

She threw up her hands in dismay. "Then I really can't go!"

Tom pulled a chair around and straddled it. His gaze on Marjorie, he folded his arms across the ladder-back. "Mom. You were supposed to go to Italy on your honeymoon. That trip got put off by financial concerns. And again when you found out you were pregnant with me. And yet again when Dad passed. Like Emma said, you've *earned* this. And the boys and I really, really want you to have it. Plus the trip is all paid for in advance, with no refunds possible." He paused to let that sink in.

The older woman's hands traced the top of her cup. "There's no way you can cancel?"

"Nope," Tom told her victoriously. "And because I knew you would be this way, I passed on the opportunity to get trip insurance. Just so you'd have to go..."

"It's unfair of you to use guilt on me," Marjorie huffed.

He laughed. "So you'll go?"

Again, his mom hesitated. "Only if you promise me that you will have backup help here the entire time to help with the boys."

"No problem."

His mother gingerly touched her bandaged forehead. "Who are you going to get?"

Now, it was Tom's turn to be at a loss.

Before she could think, Emma blurted, "Me."

Both Reids turned to look at her. Aware it was the right thing to do, she promised, "I'll make sure Tom and the boys are fine."

It was hard to figure out who looked more stunned.

"We...couldn't ask you to do that...could we?" Marjorie said, her tone registering sudden hope.

"Sure, you can. This is Laramie County, remember? Where neighbors help neighbors whenever, however they can. And Tom and I grew up together."

Marjorie snorted. "You also haven't been speaking for years and years."

"Well, it's about time for that to change, don't you-all think?" Emma returned, knowing in her heart it was true. It had been hard as heck the last eighteen months, ever since she'd returned to Laramie, trying to avoid the man who had once been the love of her life.

Life would be a whole lot easier if she didn't have to go the other way whenever they unexpectedly crossed paths.

"Well," Marjorie conceded, as a wicked glint came into her eyes, "you were awfully good with them this morning…"

Nothing so unusual about that, Emma thought. "Comes with the territory, when most of your siblings are married with kids."

Only she and her brother Travis were still single, and childless. Though Noah, sadly, was a widower.

Marjorie looked at Tom, silently seeming to inquire if he could accept such a plan.

For a long moment, his expression was maddeningly inscrutable. Then he shrugged and his face broke out in a broad grin. He stood and went over to pull his mom to her feet, where he wrapped her in a big bear hug. "Sounds like we all have ourselves a solution," he drawled. Then he gave his mother another heartfelt squeeze. "So, you better get packing…"

They all talked a little more. Then Marjorie went upstairs to conference call her gal pals, review her wardrobe and try and figure out what she was going to need. Meanwhile, Tom gathered up the coffee cups and slid them into the dishwasher. He turned to face Emma, looking as handsome and sexy as ever. His gaze drifted over her. "Want me to give you a ride back to town, so you can pick up your SUV?"

She tingled everywhere his glance had touched. Definitely a big yellow Caution sign.

She tamped down her desire and smiled. "It's not necessary. I already texted my sister Jillian, and she's going to give me a ride."

He nodded.

With nothing more to say, she grabbed her bag and headed for the front door. Tom fell into step beside her. "Thanks for talking my mom into going to Italy."

Emma let him hold the door for her. She thought about all the times he and his mom and dad had been there for her, when she and Tom were dating. In a lot of ways, even though the two of them were no longer a couple and hadn't been for some time, they still felt like family. She held his gaze sincerely. "I meant what I said. I'll help you-all out in whatever way you need."

He walked out onto the front porch beside her. "Thanks. I don't think I'll need much assistance, but it's always good to have backup in case of an emergency."

Emma caught a whiff of mint and the soap he favored. "It is."

He squinted out at the horizon. Appearing to look for Jillian's delivery truck. He leaned against one of the Craftsman-style porch pillars. "I guess I owe *you* a favor now."

Another tingle of awareness went through her, coupled with an emotional intensity that could prove dangerous to both of them.

Which was maybe why he was suddenly looking so guarded, too.

She tilted her head at him. Curious. A little resentful, too. She had been trying to be nice. Yet he was taking it down to this level.

"We're keeping score?"

He shrugged. "You went out of your way to help me, and my family, this morning. So now I'll go out of my way to help you. And lease you the space for the six-month term you requested, with an option to renew if you choose to stay."

Would she really want to do that? Realistically, it didn't seem likely. Especially if her current dream came true.

"What about letting me move in this weekend? And take the apartment as is."

He studied her contemplatively. "That's really what you want?"

"Yes, it really is."

He dipped his head in acceptance, promising, "Then we'll get it done."

Chapter Three

"Are you sure you want to do this?" Robert Lockhart asked Saturday afternoon. He paused at the rear of the small U-Haul truck Emma had rented to move her things to town, his brows knitted in concern.

Emma shut and latched the back of the vehicle. She knew her parents meant well, but they weren't making this any easier. Bracing herself for one last battle, she turned to face her father. "Yes, Dad, I am." She adopted his strong, quiet demeanor.

Carol moved closer to her rancher husband and linked her arm through his. Speaking in the soothing tones she used with her social work clients, she said, "Then at least let us help you financially, sweetheart. Maybe pay the first year's lease…?"

"I'm only going to be there for six months, Mom."

Carol countered, "But is that really enough time to get your own business going?"

"It's all the time I'm giving myself, Mom."

Her parents winced in unison.

Emma forged on. "I'll either make it by then, or I won't, in which case I'll have to accept that two years of effort is all I can afford to spend on this venture and I'll have to get a job elsewhere."

What she would *not* do was use anyone else's savings in the process.

Her parents nodded. Finally seeing there was no way to talk her out of this. "Your brothers are meeting you in town to carry your things in?" Robert asked.

"Yep. All four of them signed up to help. And Jillian and Faith are both coming to give me a hand putting my personal things away." The studio/workshop setup would come later, when she had time to unpack all her tools, machines and materials. In the meantime, though, she was going to have her own apartment again, and she was excited about that. As much as she loved her folks, she was ready to be out on her own. Smiling, she continued, "So, I should be all set."

Her mom wrapped her in a fierce hug. "You'll call us if you need anything?"

Emma hugged her parents in turn. "I promise," she said.

It took close to five hours to finish, but by the time she returned the moving truck, and said goodbye to all her sibs, who were headed home to their own families, the businesses on Main Street were shutting down for the day. And that was when she heard a knock on the door. To her surprise, she saw Tom and his three sons on the other side of the big glass windows of the first-floor storefront, hands cupped around their faces, all peering into the shadowy darkness.

She switched on the overhead lights and went to unlock the old-fashioned, beveled glass front door.

"Just wanted to make sure everything went smoothly during your move-in today," Tom said.

In jeans, a navy shirt and boots, he looked hand-some and relaxed as could be. He gave her a long, welcoming look that had her insides quivering in re-action. She edged away from the woodsy scent of his cologne, wishing she weren't quite so aware of him. "It went great." Her heart skittered in her chest. "Your mom get off on her trip okay?"

Tom nodded. "We drove her to the Dallas Fort Worth airport, and made sure she met up with her friends and got checked in for her flight to Rome."

Wishing she had a place in the store to have them sit down, Emma folded her arms in front of her. Watch-ing, while all three boys roamed the mostly empty front room that would soon be set up as a retail space. "She must be so excited."

"She said she's worried," Crockett piped up.

Austin leaned against Tom's side. He had one arm wrapped around his daddy's leg. "But not so worried," he explained to Emma solemnly, "now that she knows that you and some of the other moms—"

"In the Laramie Multiples Club," Tom explained.

"—are going to help Daddy take care of us."

So, Emma thought, he had already enlisted extra

help to take the pressure off her during the next two weeks. It was a thoughtful move. Yet sort of disturbing, too. Did he think she wasn't capable of helping him? Or just that he wouldn't be able to count on her to rise to the challenge, and really be there for him, the way she hadn't been when he had first decided to stay in Laramie and take over the family ranch.

Bowie, still focused on the information they were imparting, nodded emphatically. "Because Gramma knows Daddy can't take care of us on his own," he added.

Marjorie really needed to stop saying that, Emma thought. At least in front of the kids. Judging by the chagrined look on Tom's face, he agreed.

She smiled encouragingly at the three boys. "Your grandma will be home again before you know it. In the meantime, she is going to have a very fun vacation, and we can all be glad about that. Right?"

The triplets' heads bobbed up and down in unison. "Do you know how to make pancakes?" Crockett asked.

"'Cause we want breakfast for dinner," Bowie explained.

Scrunching his forehead, Austin added, "And Daddy says the restaurants here only serve breakfast in the morning."

"That is true," Emma said. The few brunch places they had in town closed by 2:00 p.m. The rest stuck by the traditional menus at the normal times.

Tom's phone buzzed. He pulled it out of his pocket. "Got to get this." He pressed the accept FaceTime button and Marjorie appeared on screen. "Hey, Mom." He checked his watch. "Aren't you supposed to be boarding your flight?"

Emma hoped there hadn't been a problem in customs with the older woman's passport. To her knowledge, this was the first time she had flown internationally.

"In five minutes," Marjorie said. Her three friends and travel companions lingered in the background, concern on their faces. "I just wanted to check in with you before I got on the airplane, make sure everything is fine."

Tom turned the phone around, so she could see all three of his sons, and Emma. "We're fine, as you can see. Say *buon viaggio* to Grandma, boys."

"Buon viaggio," they dutifully repeated.

Bowie's brow furrowed. "What does that mean?"

"It's how you say have a good trip in Italian," Emma explained.

Crockett reached for the phone. "Gramma, can you tell Emma how to make pancakes for us? 'Cause Daddy doesn't know how to cook!"

Marjorie immediately looked as anxious as her friends. Emma reached for the phone. "No worries. Tom and I have got this."

His mom relaxed. "I knew I could count on you," she murmured.

Her friends prodded, "Come on, Marj."

"Tom and Emma have this!"

"Time to go!"

"I'll call you when I land in Rome!" Marjorie promised. The call ended. The boys immediately looked bereft. And a little nervous, too.

Once again, Emma followed her instincts and jumped in to help. "So back to these pancakes you-all want…"

"I've never seen the kids go to sleep so fast," Tom said shortly after seven.

"Sounds like they had a really long day."

"They were up at dawn to help Mom try and fit everything in her suitcases. Which was interesting to say the least."

"Did they have to sit on them for her, so she could get them closed?"

"Yep." Tom chuckled, recalling. "Then they had the two and a half hour drive to the airport. The excitement of standing in line and seeing their grandma get checked in for her flight. Half an hour spent watching big planes land and take off. Another two and a half hour drive back to Laramie. Followed by a visit to your new store, a pancake-making lesson from you. And dinner with their new favorite lady."

They were fast making the list of her favorite kiddos, too.

Tom took his place beside her at the kitchen sink. He had rolled his sleeves up to his elbows. A dusting of hair covered his suntanned skin. Since he had helped his sons with their baths, his shirt was damp in places, clinging to his muscular chest and abs. He smelled like kid shampoo and soap, too.

Ignoring the fluttering in her middle, Emma said, "They were really sweet."

He dried the griddle, while she finished washing out the mixing bowl. "They always are when they're happy."

They exchanged fragile smiles. "Which is…how often?"

Tom's gaze held hers. "Whenever my mom is around, and apparently you as well."

His compliment meant more to her than it should. "They like women?"

He shrugged his broad shoulders. "A woman's soothing presence." He reached for another dish to dry. "Which is why my mom's sole ambition in life now seems to be to get me married off again."

She savored his nearness, and the pleasure that came from being alone with him. "And you don't concur?" she asked, curious. He had always been in a rush to cement things before.

He exhaled. "A marriage is a lot of work."

She wondered what his union had been like before his wife's death when his sons were two. She had always assumed he had been incredibly happy, the way most young, newly married couples were. Now, something in his expression made her wonder if that had been completely true. Or if there had been issues that made him reluctant to ever get hitched again.

Curious, she straightened to her full height. "And you're not interested in that?"

He met her bluntly assessing gaze. "I've got three kids, a ranch to run, and a real estate business." An inscrutable emotion flickered in his amber eyes. "No woman worth her salt would want to play second fiddle to all that."

Aware she was stricken with a sudden desire to kiss him, Emma busied herself wiping down counters. "Mmm. I don't know." Tamping down her unwanted desire, she sent him a teasing look over her shoulder. "You might be selling yourself short."

Grooves deepened on either side of his mouth. "What do you mean?" he asked in the low, flirtatious tone she loved.

Aware how easy it would be to fall for this sexy cowboy all over again, Emma ticked off his attributes with all the passion of a grocery list read out loud. "Three adorable kids. A mom who lives in and loves to help out."

"That's all?"

With effort, she forced herself to meet his probing gaze. Aware the air between them was quickly becoming way too palpable, she shrugged, adding, "Financial security."

He leaned in close, mimicking her low tone perfectly. "Nothing else going for me...?"

She swallowed around the sudden parched feeling in her throat. Aware if she wanted to, she could come up with a heck of a lot more. But, not wanting him to know how incredibly attractive she still found him, she merely inclined her head at him, feigning an insouciance she couldn't begin to really feel. "Fishing for compliments, cowboy?"

"Why not?" His expression became even more mischievous. "Unless you can't think of anything more." He seemed to be daring her to try.

Refusing to let his needling get under her skin, she said, "You're not too bad to look at."

"Good to know." Masculine satisfaction tautening the rugged planes of his face, he wrapped his arms around her waist. Pulled her close.

The tips of her breasts brushed the hardness of his chest. "Neither are you," he whispered against her ear.

Emma caught her breath. "What are you doing?"

He wrapped one hand around the nape of her neck; the other flattened on her spine. Then his eyes shuttered to half-mast as his head slowly dipped toward hers. "Testing the waters."

She shivered as his lips ghosted lightly over hers. "I'm not sure—" yearning swept through her, fierce and undeniable "—we should be…"

But already her eyes were closing, too. Already she was losing herself in the emotions of the past. In the feel of his hard, warm body pressed against hers. The passion he conjured up so easily. The implacable masculine taste of his mouth. The warm stroking of his palm down her spine. The resolute possession of his lips claiming hers…

She thought she knew what it was like to be kissed by him.

She didn't.

Not like this. As if he wanted to get to know her all over again, and savor every inch of her, heart and soul.

Need swept through her. Fierce. Undeniable. It had been so long since she had been kissed, touched, held.

So long since anyone had wanted her like this. The way he always had. Her whole body trembled, radiating heat, and he responded by kissing her even more thoroughly. Unable to help herself, she surged against him. And still they kissed. Hard and fast. Slow and easy. Softly. Tenderly. Erotically.

The years melted away.

Emma lost herself in him and the moment, just the way she used to.

Only things weren't the same, she reminded herself reluctantly. Might never be.

Realizing how much she was beginning to want him, and vice versa, she splayed her hands across his chest and pulled away. He continued looking at her. As if waiting for her to tell him what was on her mind. She drew a stabilizing breath. "As much as I enjoyed spending time with you, and would like to be friends with you again, I think it's a mistake to want anything more than that."

Frustration warred with the determination on his face. "So, no more kisses?"

She released a beleaguered sigh, knowing one thing for certain. She could not settle for less than what they had once had. And he shouldn't either. No matter how fierce the passion shimmering between them was. "Not if we're smart. No."

The following afternoon, Emma's sister Mackenzie drove in from Fort Worth, with the sign that Emma had commissioned. Her brother Travis, a part-time cowboy and full-time contractor slash handyman, also showed up to help with the installation.

Mackenzie was happily married, with twins. Travis had gone through a broken engagement, and was still single and childless, like her. All three of them were entrepreneurs although her siblings were both more financially successful.

So far, anyway.

"So let me get this straight," Mackenzie murmured, as she and Emma caught up on the events of the past couple of days, while their brother got his tools and a ladder out of the back of his pickup truck. "You had a great time with Tom and his kids, and then you kissed him. Sparks flew. So, you felt you had no choice but to put him in the strictly-friends zone?"

"Ouch," Travis murmured, catching the last part of it. "Talk about stomping on a man's ego!"

Emma glared at her brother. "No need to worry about that. Tom Reid's ego is just fine!"

"Glad to hear that," a low voice rumbled from behind her.

Emma whirled around to see Tom striding toward her, another ladder in hand. "What are you doing here?" she gasped. "And where are the triplets?"

"The fellas are at a playdate at Mitzy Martin McCabe's house, with her quadruplet sons."

Emma gaped. "*Seven* preschool boys, all together?"

He waved off her concern. "Chase is there to help manage it. And when the seven boys are together, they are pretty much self-entertaining. They usually have too much fun to get into trouble."

Mitzy's CEO husband was a very capable guy, and great with kids. Dryly, Emma returned, "Good to know, I guess. But that doesn't explain what you are doing here."

One corner of his sensual mouth lifted. "Me and my giant ego, you mean?"

Emma tipped her chin at him, correcting archly, "I never said giant."

He quirked a brow, apparently not about to let her off the hook. "It was implied."

Mackenzie and Travis chuckled.

She felt herself flush self-consciously. "Answer my question, please, cowboy."

Mackenzie couldn't resist playfully upping the stakes. "Don't you mean Wheeler-Dealer Cowboy? That is what you used to call Tom when you were kids."

"Only because it fit, and still does."

"Ohhhh-ho!" her siblings crowed in unison.

Appearing satisfied he had gotten her full attention, Tom's glance turned serious. "Travis figured he would need help with the sign installation, and he called me earlier to see if I was available, and I am."

"Thanks, man." Travis slapped Tom's palm. Tom slapped Travis's in return.

"So, let's see it," Tom said.

Mackenzie removed the protective covering.

THE BOOT LAB, CUSTOM SHOES AND BOOTS BY EMMA LOCKHART was painted in fire-engine red within a fancy black-edged ribbon, on a white background.

Emma had seen the mock-up of the finished product, but nothing compared to seeing it in person. "Oh my gosh, Mackenzie, it's gorgeous!" She hugged her sister. "Thank you so much!"

"Glad you like it," Mackenzie murmured, embracing her back.

Tom continued studying it with a fellow businessperson's critical eye. He, too, seemed impressed. "I like the logo," he said finally. "It's going to look really nice against the red brick storefront."

"Impressive," Travis agreed.

All business once again, Tom said, "Now let's get it put up."

The next half an hour was spent figuring out just exactly where the sign should be placed, and getting the brackets centered. Finally, it was up. All four of them stepped back to admire the work.

Tom turned to her with a smile. "Congratulations."

Emma resisted the urge to throw herself into his arms and accept the hug he seemed to want to give. "Thank you," she said. Even though she knew it really shouldn't matter to her how he felt about her business since they were no longer together.

As their eyes met, the moment drew out, and she felt a wave of warmth spread through her chest.

Mackenzie waited until Tom turned to gather up his tools, then whispered in her ear, "I'd rethink that friend zone thing if I were you." Emma elbowed her sister.

Tom who hadn't been able to hear what was said, gave them a perplexed look. Meanwhile, Travis focused on the big blue bus headed slowly down the street. As it came closer, the uniformed driver seemed to be checking the numbers on the buildings. The bus stopped next to them. The driver put the vehicle in park, and opened the door with a whoosh. "Any of you know a—" he glanced at the clipboard in his hands "—Miss Emma Lockhart?"

Surprised, she lifted her hand. "That's me!"

The driver grinned. "Wait right there, miss. I've got a gift for you from the Rossi family in Le Marche, Italy." He handed over an envelope.

Inside, was the familiar handwriting of the senior Rossi. It said simply:

Darling Emma,
This is the beginning of all your dreams coming true.

Mackenzie peered over Emma's shoulder. "Well, I like the sound of that," she said.

"You'll like what comes next even more." The driver signaled.

Another uniformed attendant stepped forward, toting a wire crate. Together, they brought it down the steps of the bus and onto the sidewalk.

"This is Buttercup," the attendant said, nodding at the curly haired Australian labradoodle inside. "And she is all yours. If you accept delivery of her, that is."

Emma knelt and looked at the trembling dog, so shocked and delighted she didn't know what to say. Nor did anyone else. Although Tom looked as if he were already as in love with the pup as she was.

"We drove her all the way from Wisconsin," the attendant said.

For the first time, Emma paid attention to the writing on the side of the bus: Luxury Pet Transport, for All 48 States.

"So, she is a little tired and confused, but she's a great dog," the attendant continued.

"How old?" Emma asked.

"Two years, three months and five days, according to her papers."

Emma guessed the pet weighed about forty-five pounds or so. Which was in her estimation the perfect size. Not too big, not too small...

"So, do you want her? The Rossis felt sure you would, even if it was a surprise."

Emma's heart swelled with love, even as beneath that, other more complex emotions simmered. "Of course, I want her," she said. Who turned down an adorable pet? Especially when it was the exact breed she had always wanted!

"Here are all Buttercup's papers, and information, food, training treats and a favorite toy." The driver carried down a pet travel bag.

"Just sign here." The attendant held out the papers.

Emma did.

She received the leash.

And moments later, the bus drove off.

Emma handed Tom the leash. "Just in case we have a runner," she said.

He smiled, as much an animal lover as she was. "Happy to be your backup."

Aware she was glad to be able to rely on his strong, steady presence again, at least for the moment, she knelt on the sidewalk.

Buttercup was now at the back of her crate, looking at them with big, dark brown eyes. Emma gently opened the door, while Tom hunkered down beside her. "Come here, sweetheart," she said, her arms outstretched.

And slowly, Buttercup did. Not stopping until she had happily greeted them both.

Chapter Four

"Thanks for letting the boys play with Buttercup this evening," Tom told Emma, hours later.

She turned toward him. With the boys asleep upstairs, moonlight shining overhead and Buttercup exploring the fenced backyard, it was a surprisingly peaceful spring evening. As their eyes locked, she realized how much more there was to the handsome rancher these days than just an ability to negotiate a good business deal or make mind-blowing love. He was a devoted dad to his kids. A good son to his mom. Fun to be around. Even kinder and more generous than she recalled.

Had they not already proved once that they were spectacularly wrong for each other, he might have been the perfect man for her.

Unfortunately, their divergent goals still existed.

He would always be staying here, in Laramie County, with the life he already knew and loved.

Whereas she was still looking to fulfill an ambition that would likely have her moving elsewhere in six months...

Plus, he had indicated he did not want to get married again. Because it was "a lot of work" and he already had too much on his agenda.

And she really did want to get married and have a family of her own some day. When the time and the man were right.

Which meant they had to keep things casual.

Determined to stay the course, she flashed him a grateful smile. "Thanks for inviting 'us' to a takeout pizza dinner." The tender adulation of Tom and his boys had gone a long way toward helping the Australian labradoodle settle in, after her cross-country bus ride.

His eyes crinkled at the corners. "No problem. It was the least we could do after the way you've helped us out this week."

Liking the fact, they were back to supporting each other, in the same way they had from childhood on, she said, "My pleasure."

Together, they watched Buttercup explore the grass around the boys' big wooden swing set and play fort.

Tom had rolled up his sleeves again, to just below his elbow. Their forearms brushed lightly as they settled on the cushioned glider on the stone patio. Emma ignored the tingling sensation, even as her heartbeat picked up.

He cocked a brow, his glance drifting over her lazily. "So what is it about the Rossis' gift that bothers you?" he asked.

"What do you mean?"

He shrugged. "She's a beautiful dog. Well-trained. And affectionate. And it's clear she took to you as readily as you took to her, yet...you keep frowning every time you look at her." He squinted at her thoughtfully. "Are you worried about the inconvenience of having Buttercup in town, in a second-floor apartment? When you're trying to run a business down below?"

She tilted her head, and their glances clashed once again. He hadn't shaved since that morning, and the stubble of beard lining his strong jaw gave him a ruggedly handsome look. She drew a breath and took a sip of the sparkling water she'd brought outside with her. "Not at all."

"Then what is it? The fact that the Rossi family didn't ask if you even wanted a dog before they sent you Buttercup?"

Trying not to think how cozy it felt sitting with him like this, Emma shook her head. "No."

His glance narrowed. "Then...?"

Why could he still read her so easily? Shouldn't he have lost that ability by now? "It's...complicated."

He shifted in his seat, the hardness of his knee pressing against hers in the process. "I'm listening."

Emma sighed. He had always known when something was bothering her. Maybe she *should* talk about this, at least a little bit. "If I say it out loud, I'm going to sound ungrateful."

"And if you don't," Tom countered, "and continue to keep whatever is bothering you all bottled up inside, then your new pet is going to feel it."

She did not want that. Buttercup had already had too much upheaval in her life in the past few days. The last thing she wanted to do was add to the dog's stress. "It's just that the gift feels like some kind of consolation prize. Like an admission of guilt on their part. And they have nothing to feel sorry about."

He draped his arm over the back of the glider. "Now I really don't get it."

Resisting the urge to snuggle in his arms, Emma let out a slow breath. "You're sure you want to hear all this?"

Something shifted in his expression. "I want to hear everything about your life when we were apart."

She could understand that. She wanted to catch up on what had gone on with him, too. Maybe it would help them to talk openly and honestly.

"The Rossi family shoe company is a four-generation business in Le Marche. They started it from nothing and have grown it into a multimillion-dollar enterprise that has shops in Europe and North America. They regularly outfit celebrities and royalty, as well as the very rich. They are also very effusive and generous with their knowledge and time." She cleared her throat. "They really took me under their wing when I started apprenticing with them. Made me feel like a member of their family and told me I always would have a place with them."

"And you felt the same way about them, I gather?"

"I adored everyone, from the great-grandfather to the toddlers running around. And I saw a lot of them, because the other apprentices and I lived in cottages on their estate. But, at the same time, I missed my own family. I was homesick for Texas. Felt I was missing out on way too much here…"

A look of compassion filling his eyes, he waited for her to continue.

"So, when it came to the end of my apprenticeship, I didn't have a 'what's next' discussion with them, the way some of my other coworkers did. I didn't want to hear what they were going to offer me, because I knew I was leaving. They understood my need to be back in Texas again, and that was that." She released a shuddering breath. "Although they did tell me that if I ever changed my mind and wanted to go back to Italy, that I would always have a place with them."

"And you did go back to see them, last January," Tom recalled.

"Yes. I was really embarrassed about the way the deal I had been working on with that high-end bridal salon had fallen apart. But I believed in my handmade wedding boot. I had over one hundred testimonials from brides who had worn them. And I knew if I could get the right marketing and distribution that I would have a success on my hands. So, I offered them my design."

"And?"

Miserably, she related, "They were horrified by the depth of the misunderstanding between us. When they had said I would always be family to them, they had meant it, but as for the Rossi business...that was for actual Rossi family members only. They did the designs, and owned the styles, patents, copyrights and licensing agreements."

His lips tightened. "So they never planned to offer you a job?"

Mortification made her cheeks flame. "Not as an executive. Or designer. Just a shoemaker."

He covered her hand with his. "And you were...?"

"Hurt. Humiliated. Embarrassed. I stayed another day, but it was so awkward that I made up an excuse about one of my sisters needing me and flew home early."

Tom studied her kindly. "So, you think they gave you a dog as some sort of consolation prize?"

Emma nodded. "I know they felt bad about our gigantic misunderstanding. I did, too. I never would have put them on the spot like that if I had understood the limits of our friendship. The fact that what worked within the boundaries of my apprenticeship was not going to be anywhere near as viable when it ended."

"Does your family know about this?"

"Heavens, no." Aware she and Tom were getting a little too cozy, she withdrew her hand from his, stood and began to pace. "They were embarrassed enough when my deal with that high-end boutique fell through. If they knew about another failed pitch, and misjudgment on my part..."

He stood, too. "You think they wouldn't have supported you?"

Emma threw up her hands in frustration. Pivoted away. "*I* almost can't support this dream anymore."

He moved so she had no choice but to look at him. Swallowing a lump in her throat, she admitted, "If it hadn't been for the email I received from the head buyer of the Ready To Wear Bridal chain asking to tour my studio and talk about this super comfy yet elegant wedding boot they were hearing about, I might have already thrown in the towel."

He cupped her shoulders between his palms. "That would have been a mistake."

She leaned into his warm, reassuring touch. "You really think so?"

He nodded, his hold becoming even more intimate. "You can't give up when you're this close," he told her in the tender-gruff voice she loved. "Not after all the hard work you've done."

She searched his face, not knowing why his support meant so much to her, just knowing that it did. She wrinkled her nose at him. "You haven't even seen my designs."

He looked down at her feet. "You're wearing one right now, aren't you?"

The engineer boot had a two-inch stack heel, and was made of the finest dark brown leather, perfect for casual wear. It paired wonderfully with jeans. "Yes."

His attention returning to her face, he offered a slow, sexy smile. "They're nice."

"Thanks," she whispered.

Their eyes locked and held. All too soon, he let go of her shoulders. She felt instantly bereft. He continued talking about shoes and all she could think about was how nice it would be to kiss him again, just for a minute...

Buttercup ambled over to them. She lay down in the grass next to Emma. "Tired, baby?" she crooned, stroking her new pet's silky golden head.

Buttercup sighed and rolled over onto her side. She got the hint and rubbed her chest and belly with long, gentle strokes. Buttercup settled in, as if to go to sleep.

Without warning, Emma found herself yawning, too.

She rose reluctantly. "I better drive into town."

Tom slanted her a questioning look. "You sure you want to do that when I have a perfectly good guest room here? One," he coaxed before she could interrupt, "you've slept in before."

Emma drew a bolstering breath. She looked around for the leash, then realized she must have left it inside the ranch house. "When we were dating and engaged."

Together, the three of them headed back.

Tom gallantly let both females go first. "Which is not a prerequisite for anyone who wants to sleep in that bed."

She listed the first of many reasons why not. "I don't have pajamas."

He shrugged, amber eyes twinkling. "You can borrow one of my button-downs."

The way she had when they had been in college.

All sorts of sexy images danced in her head. The

yearning to make love to him grew. She cleared her throat. "Probably not a good idea, either."

"It's better than you getting behind the wheel when you're this wiped out. Never mind having to haul a wire crate, a suitcase full of pet paraphernalia and a dog up to the second-floor apartment, via stairs.

"Plus you don't know how Buttercup is going to do this first night in a new place. If you're going to have to get dressed to take her out repeatedly in the wee hours of the morning…"

He did have a point about that.

She did want to stay.

But only on *her* terms. Emma braced her hands on her hips while her dog leaned tiredly against her calf. "How about this? Buttercup and I will take you up on your offer if you let us have the sofa in the living room. So, if we need to go out, we can slip in and out without disturbing anyone."

He nodded reluctantly. "Clothes…?"

She kept her guard up. Letting him know with a quelling look, "I won't be wearing any of yours."

He snapped his fingers in disappointment, grinning.

What were they doing? Starting to flirt like this? Emma forced herself to get it together. She stepped closer, talking in a low voice that would not carry up the stairs. "Seriously, I will just wear what I have on right now, sans my boots."

He accompanied her to the formal living room, where a long sofa awaited. Taking a cue from her, he stepped the sexiness down a notch. Although the long-held affection in his eyes remained. "Toothbrush?" he said, just as softly.

She gestured at her bag, on the foyer table. "Always carry one and a small tube of paste in my purse for emergencies."

"Wow. You do come prepared."

She refused to let herself succumb to his sexy drawl. Saying only, "Cowboy, you have no idea."

Tom carried Buttercup's travel crate in from her car and set it next to the living room sofa. By the time Emma had put Buttercup to bed with a treat, he had returned with a blanket and pillow. He, too, looked a little tired around the eyes. Reminding her that he'd had a very long weekend, too. His gaze touched her hair and cheeks before returning to her eyes. "Needless to say, if you want anything, help yourself," he told her in a low, gravelly tone.

"Thanks." Struggling against the urge to kiss him, she stepped back to give him a wide berth. "Well…" She feigned a huge yawn. "See you in the morning."

He moved back, too, the perfect gentleman now. "Good night." Turning, he headed across the foyer, up the staircase. Once again, she was alone. Which was likely the way it would stay, if she focused solely on her career, as planned.

Emma thought she would go right to sleep. She didn't. Being at the Rocking R reminded her of all the times she had spent there in years past. How happy she had been before her and Tom's breakup. The rational side of her knew she could not erase the past, or turn back the clock. But the emotional side of her was still wishing for just that as she and her new pet drifted off to sleep.

The next thing she knew she was waking up again. This time, to the sound of youthful arguing.

"You can't wake her up!" Crockett hissed.

"Daddy said we got to let her sleep!" Bowie agreed.

"And anyway," Austin said, "she looks like a fairy-tale princess, so only a prince can wake her up with a kiss. You know, like in those movies Gramma likes."

"But then they'd fall in love and get married," Bowie said.

"Which would be good," Crockett countered, "because then we could probably have breakfast for dinner every day." It was all Emma could do to stifle a laugh.

"Is she smiling?" Austin stage-whispered.

"Maybe she's just having a good dream," Bowie said.

Or a good way to wake up, Emma thought. Surrounded by Tom's lively and adorable sons.

Without warning, an ache went through her. Times like this, she really missed having kids and a husband of her own.

"Boys!" Tom barked from a distance away. "I thought I told you not to go in here!"

Aware the time to play possum had ended, Emma roused herself enough to open her eyes and sit up. "It's okay." She held up a staying palm. "I'm awake."

His gaze roved her, head to toe. Taking in her sleepy state. He had already shaved and showered. His dark hair was rumpled and wet. He smelled like the masculine soap and mint toothpaste he favored.

Alert, too, Buttercup let out a little whine and sat up in her crate. "How about the boys and I give you a moment," Tom suggested kindly, "while we take Buttercup outside to relieve herself?"

Emma began folding the blanket she'd slept under. Finished, she put it on the back of the sofa. "Great idea. Thank you."

By the time they had all come back in, she had Buttercup's food and water set out in the kitchen. And was rummaging around in the fridge. "You-all want me to cook you some breakfast? Maybe some breakfast tacos?"

"Yes! Please!" the three boys said in unison.

"But we only like cheese and egg in ours," Bowie explained.

Tom smiled. "I'll have the same."

"Coming right up." Aware this was what her mornings would be like if she did have a family of her own one day, Emma set a large skillet on the stove and began cracking eggs into a mixing bowl.

"Do we have to go to school today?" Crockett asked Tom with a scowl.

"Yeah, I don't want to be in a different class," Bowie said.

"Me, neither," Austin agreed. "It will be too lonely without my brothers."

"Well, that's probably true," Emma said when their dad seemed not to know how to respond.

Tom gave her an *are you kidding me* look.

Ignoring his silent censure, still whisking the eggs, she continued talking to his sons in the same genial tone. "On the other hand, if you are all in different classes, you will all get to do different things and play with different kids. And then you can tell each other all about it when you do get home."

They thought about that.

Crockett sighed. "I'd still rather stay home."

"Me, too," Bowie said.

"Me, three," Austin agreed.

But they all seemed resigned that they were going to have to go to school, so they stopped arguing about it.

Tom handed Emma the shredded Monterey Jack– cheddar cheese blend and got out the flour tortillas.

"Who wants salsa for their tacos?" he asked, reminding Emma what a good team they had once made.

"Me," Crockett said.

"I want maple syrup," Austin declared.

"Ketchup," said Bowie. "Please."

To Emma's surprise, the boys not only dunked their tacos in the various condiments, they really enjoyed them, scarfing down two each.

"Will you be here when we get home from school?" Austin wanted to know.

"Actually, I have to work today, so I'll be in town," Emma told them gently.

Three faces turned very sad.

She realized they were probably missing their grandmother a lot. Especially since this was the first and only time Marjorie had actually left them for more than a few hours at a time. "But maybe your dad could drop by with you after school and you could see my design studio. How about that?"

"Can we, Daddy?" Crockett asked.

Tom gratefully met her eyes. "It sounds like a lot of fun to me." Without warning, he gave her a one-armed hug, the impulsive, affectionate kind you give a friend. "Thanks," he whispered in her ear. He squeezed her again, and let her go.

"You're welcome," Emma said.

And knew, even before his sensual lips curved into a smile, that her attempts to keep him in the friend zone just weren't going to work.

Chapter Five

"So what do you think?" Emma's brother Travis asked later that same day. "Is this going to be the right size display stand or not?"

She looked at the three-tiered wooden square he had built for her. Indecision rippled through her. "I'm not sure," she admitted candidly. "I thought it was going to be the perfect dimension, but now I don't know if it is going to be large enough."

Emma always found it easy to talk to her brother. A decade older than her, he had been the last of the eight siblings to be adopted by Carol and Robert Lockhart, after their birth parents perished in a tragic accident. Whereas she, then an infant, had been the very first.

Travis continued surveying the space. "How many displays were you going to have?"

"Seven. Four for the front and three staggered in the row behind that." She drew a breath, trying to tamp down her anxiety about the pending visit from the buyer at RTW Bridal. "I want to have enough room to be able to walk around all four sides of each one comfortably."

Her brother got out his measuring tape. "Well, then I don't think you're going to want to go much larger. Adding even four inches in diameter is going to cut down on the aisleways. You don't want your customers to feel crowded."

"You're right." Emma decided. "Let's just stick with what I initially ordered from you. Can you still get it done ASAP?"

"Yep. In fact, I will probably be ready to start putting things together in here by the end of this week."

She sighed her relief. "That's great. Thank you!"

Travis hooked his metal measuring tape back onto his belt. "You okay?" he asked. "I've been to plenty of trunk shows with you and helped you set up, and it's not like you to be so indecisive."

"I know…" She thought about her fast-dwindling bank account. "But I have a lot riding on this."

Travis continued to study her, as if he were wondering if that was all it was.

Or if it could have something to do with Tom. And his re-entrance into her life.

A rap sounded on the display window at the front of the store. Emma turned to see two residents of Laramie Gardens, the home for seniors, grinning broadly at her. Miss Mim had been the town librarian for fifty years, and was as flashily dressed as always. Beside her was Miss Isabelle, looking chic and elegant as per usual. Both were carrying shopping bags bearing Main Street store logos.

"Can we come in?" they shouted through the window.

Emma went to open the door. "Sure." She smiled fondly at the ladies, who had watched her grow up. "But I'm not open for business yet, so I'm not sure what there is to see."

Miss Mim set her bags down on the gleaming wood floor. "When will you be open?"

"Two weeks from today. Limited hours. Although I'll also be taking appointments."

Miss Isabelle put her shopping bags down, as well. She beamed happily as she looked around. "What about tours of your design studio? Will you be giving those?"

"Um… I hadn't thought about it."

Miss Mim grinned, her enthusiasm apparent. "The ladies of Laramie Gardens would love to take one when your workshop is set up."

Travis turned to her. An entrepreneur himself, Emma knew he understood the pros and cons. "It would be a good way to gin up some additional business," he said.

True, she thought.

"I'll find out how many women are interested and get back to you," Miss Mim promised. She stepped forward to hug Emma. "We are so proud of you, darling!"

Miss Isabelle embraced her, too. "And we can't wait to try on some of your footwear!"

Spying someone on the street, Miss Mim waved, as if inviting them in also.

The door jangled once again, and Tom and his triplets walked in. The boys looked grumpy and out of sorts. Their dad looked desperate for help. Emma's heart went out to them.

"Hello, fellas!" Miss Mim's cheerful voice rang out.

"How are you-all doing?" Miss Isabelle asked.

Three lower lips shot out. "Bad," Crockett fumed, stomping his foot.

Miss Mim nodded consolingly. "Missing your grandmother Marjorie, I imagine?"

"She's been gone forever," Bowie lamented.

"Actually," Tom put in meaningfully, "just two days."

Austin looked on the verge of tears. He folded his arms. "Yeah, well, I want her to come back from Italy *right now*!"

"We know you miss her," Emma soothed, stepping forward and gathering the boys in a group hug.

Meanwhile, the resolutely single Travis, who avoided domestic drama whenever possible, collected his things. He tipped his hat at the gathering crowd. "Everyone, I have to run."

Goodbyes were said, and then her sibling slipped out the door, looking as relieved to leave as Tom was to be there with her.

Miss Mim turned back to the boys, who were still staring glumly around at the empty space. She pulled a Sugar Love bakery box from one of her bags. "You know what might help you-all feel better if your daddy agrees?"

Obviously seeing where this was going, Tom nodded his permission.

"Freshly baked cookies!" Miss Mim said.

"But we probably should enjoy them on the bench outside, in front of the store," Miss Isabelle added. "So we don't get crumbs all over Miss Emma's shiny new floors."

"Can we, Daddy?" Austin asked eagerly, no longer near tears.

"We'll keep a good eye on them," Miss Mim promised.

He nodded his permission. "As long as you are good listeners and say please and thank you to Miss Mim and Miss Isabelle, you can go."

"Aren't you coming?" Bowie asked.

Tom looked at Emma. "I have to talk to Emma for a minute."

Miss Mim lit up, like the natural matchmaker she was. "You-all take your time," she said encouragingly with a wink.

"Bad day at school?" Emma asked sympathetically once the two older woman and the kids slipped out and they were alone.

"They didn't like being in separate pre-K classes, but like their teachers said, they are going to be split up in kindergarten, per school policy, next fall, so it's probably best they start getting used to it now."

"I'm sure tomorrow will be better. But, in any event, did you need me to help you tonight?"

"Actually, that is what I wanted to talk to you about." Tom smiled as Buttercup, who'd been dozing on her dog bed in the other room, joined them. "I think I've got it covered."

Sharp disappointment rolled through her. "You're sure?"

He nodded. "They have to understand that their grandmother is entitled to more of a life than she's had the past couple of years, and that the four of us can manage on our own."

Okay, that made sense. He wasn't pushing her away. Just trying to help his boys be more independent on all counts. So they wouldn't only be facing the challenge at school.

He flexed his broad shoulders. All commanding Texas cowboy once again. He looked her in the eye. Winked. "We're Reid men, after all."

"Strong and steady?" she teased.

His eyes clouded over slightly. The way they had when they'd been talking about how much work marriage could be. "Definitely what we're aiming for, but yeah."

She wondered if he was thinking about his late wife again, then decided it really wasn't any of her business. And pushed aside her surprising need to be involved in this situation. Yes, she had promised Marjorie she would help, but they also had to want her there. Apparently, Tom wanted to manage solo tonight. If only to demonstrate to his boys they could do anything they collectively set their minds to.

"Okay, well, call me if you change your mind and decide you could use some extra assistance."

"I will," he said. But even as he promised, she knew he wouldn't. One way or another, he and his sons would power through. Without her.

Emma turned to Buttercup after everyone left. "Looks like we have the whole evening ahead of us," she said, hunkering down to pet her labradoodle's silky golden curls. "Which is good, because we still have a whole lot to do to get the studio set up."

For the next three and a half hours, she opened up moving boxes and brought out patterns she had made for her shoes, and all the different kinds of threads and glues. She arranged them on the floor-to-ceiling shelves that Travis had set up for her earlier in what would be her design studio slash workroom.

Smiling, she stepped back to admire her handiwork. Tail wagging, Buttercup stood beside her. "Looks better already, doesn't it?" she mused, as her cell phone buzzed.

"Uh-oh," she said, as she saw the person making the FaceTime request. She punched the button to accept the call. "Marjorie, hi."

Tom's mother burst into tears.

"What's wrong?" Emma asked in alarm. Had something awful happened in Italy? The tour had barely started!

"I thought you were going to help see the boys were all right!" Marjorie accused.

"They are," Emma said. Then stopped as panic set in. Had something happened out at the Rocking R ranch she had yet to hear about? "Aren't they?"

Marjorie sniffed. "I just talked to them. Not only are none of them bathed and in their pj's, as they should be, because tomorrow is a school day, but they are all just miserable. They're hungry and they hate school now, and…" The older woman choked back a sob.

Okay. So, this was just separation anxiety. Realizing she needed to feed Buttercup and herself, too, Emma went to get the dog's food bowl. "Was Tom there?"

"Yes," Marjorie huffed.

Emma measured kibble, while still talking. Then knelt to put the dish in front of Buttercup. "What did he say about what's going on?"

"That he's handling it. But he is clearly not. I'm going to have to cut my trip short and come home. But I can't get a flight…"

"And you probably won't be able to on short notice, either," Emma cut in calmly. "International flights are always booked way in advance."

Marjorie wiped her eyes. "Why aren't you helping him with the boys?" she demanded.

Now it was Emma's turn to feel resentful. "I was! *Am!* They were here after school, and I made breakfast for them this morning…and dinner last night…"

Marjorie's three friends murmured something in the background. Whatever they were saying did not really seem to help. Emma knew what would. She put up a hand before Marjorie could interrupt. "Look, I can be out there in twenty minutes. In fact, Buttercup—" who had just finished her meal "—and I will head out there right now."

Marjorie blinked. "Buttercup?" she repeated in confusion.

"My new dog." In explanation, Emma turned the camera toward the labradoodle, who wagged her tail.

Marjorie smiled through her tears, while Emma turned their attention back to the trouble at hand. She reached for her carryall and the leash.

"And if we need reinforcements when I get there, then I'll call my folks to come over and help."

The older woman finally started to calm down. Although she was still on the edge of another crying jag. "Oh, thank you, Emma." She sniffed. "I really don't want to come home. But…"

Agreeing it would be a bad idea, Emma told her firmly, "Then don't cut your trip short, Marjorie!" She paused to let her words sink in. "Give Tom a chance to be the daddy those boys of his need!"

Marjorie took a deep breath. Looking faintly hopeful at long last. "Text me when you get there?"

"I will. I promise, everything will be fine."

Except it wasn't fine when she got there and Tom answered the door. With his shirt untucked and smeared with…*syrup*? He looked frazzled and as unhappy as the children she could hear yelling in the background.

"Thank God," he said, cupping his hand beneath

her elbow and drawing her and Buttercup inside his home. "I was just about to call you."

Emma set her bag and car keys on the foyer table. She texted Marjorie. "I'm here!" Then put her phone down, next to her bag. "Your mother beat you to the punch."

"I figured." He led her toward the back of the ranch house. Crockett was lying face down in the center of the family room, pounding the rug with his fists. "I don't want to go to bed!" he yelled.

"Me...neither!" Bowie rhythmically kicked at a leg of the coffee table.

Even Austin was in the throes of a meltdown. "I want my gramma to come home now!" he shouted, and promptly burst into tears. His brothers joined in.

Buttercup leaned against Emma's leg, taking it all in. Tom gave her a besieged look, completely at a loss. "How long have they been like this?" she asked.

He gestured distractedly. "It wasn't good before my mom called—they've been impossible all evening— but seeing her get so emotional really set them off."

Emma handed the leash to their frazzled dad, then hunkered down between the triplets. "Boys," she said, "you-all are scaring Buttercup!"

They paused.

"Look at her!" Emma pointed. "She is very worried. I think you're going to have to pet her and tell her that everything is going to be okay."

Austin sniffed. "Even if it isn't?"

Crockett sat up and put his hand out in wordless invitation. Buttercup moved toward him. She cuddled against him and a lovefest ensued. Soon Austin and Bowie joined in. All three petted the dog tenderly. Before long, the kind of calmness that could only come from an outpouring of love descended.

"Did you have dinner?" she asked, recalling what Marjorie had said about her grandchildren being hungry, as well as upset.

Bowie pouted. "Daddy made it, and it was icky."

"They weren't the right kind of waffles," Crockett explained.

Tom made a cut sign, so Emma moved on. Next subject. "Well—" she sat down beside the boys, and petted Buttercup, too "—you know, I'm kind of hungry, because I haven't even had any dinner yet." She made a great show of thinking of possible solutions for their dilemma. Then searched all three small faces. "I don't suppose," she said wistfully, "that you-all have some cereal and milk, do you?"

Austin leaped up. "We have five kinds!" he told her proudly. "I'll show you!"

And that was all it took to get them calmly sitting at the farmhouse-style kitchen table. By the time the boys had finished their second bowls of crunchy cereal, their heads were drooping. "Time for bed," Tom said.

They did not argue.

"Good night boys," Emma said from her place at the kitchen table.

Austin paused to look back at her. "Will you be here for breakfast tomorrow morning?" he asked.

There was no other answer to give. "Yes, I will," she promised.

* * *

Fifteen minutes later, Tom stood in the doorway of the kitchen, drinking Emma in.

He had fantasized about her being here like this many times, after they had broken up. And again, after he had lost his wife. He never thought it would happen. Yet here she was, in jeans and a formfitting T-shirt and sneakers, looking delectably tousled after what had to have been a very long weekend for her.

Green eyes sparkling with life, she sent a look toward the second floor. "They're awfully quiet."

Tom smiled and moved closer, drinking in the citrusy, orange blossom scent she favored. Her lashes were long, cheeks pink, her lips soft and bare. Desire sifted through him. "They were asleep the instant their heads hit the pillows."

Emma slid the last of the dishes into the dishwasher. Then turned to face him. Aware, as was he, that they were close enough to kiss, she stepped back. "What happened here tonight?" She indicated the smears of butter and pancake syrup across the granite countertops, the table and the floor surrounding it.

Tom grabbed the spray cleaner and paper towels. He knelt to address the floor first. Emma tackled the countertops. "I had the bright idea to buy frozen waffles and breakfast sandwiches and omelets in the freezer section of the grocery store. I figured that way we could have something different every night that was still breakfast for dinner and all I would have to do was put it in the microwave." Finished with the floor, he walked over and threw the damp and sticky towels in the trash.

Emma moved to the kitchen table, her arm outstretched in front of her as she wiped it down, too. "I'm guessing they didn't care for the waffles?"

Tom tried not to notice how her tee shifted against her breasts, molding their soft curves. Her jeans did equally nice things for her curvy hips and lissome thighs.

Ignoring the pressure at the front of his jeans, he closed the trash sack and put it next to the back door to take out later. Reminding himself that she was just here as a favor to his mom, and to help his boys, he returned to line the tall kitchen can with a new plastic bag. The guilt that he had once again let his family down again was returning. Only now it wasn't just his late wife he had failed but his three kids.

Aware Emma was still listening intently, he continued his tale of woe matter-of-factly. "The kids pointed out that my mom makes hers in the waffle iron, not the toaster, so they refused to even try them."

Emma sat down at the table, propping her chin on her upturned hand. Sensing there was much more to this story, she prodded lightly, "And then what happened?"

"I got the waffle iron out and put them in that, thinking the waffles could just heat up in there, but they got all squished and burned and then the boys were really upset."

She winced. "I can imagine."

Tom took the chair next to hers. "Which is when my

mother called. And then they went into full-fledged temper tantrums, the kind I haven't seen since my wife died."

The memory, along with the ever present wish he'd been able to do something to prevent her death, was enough to make his heart clench. He gazed into Emma's kind eyes, admitting with a sigh, "I am pretty sure that was what my mother was thinking, too. Which was what set *her* off." Making the situation even more miserable. "And then the boys cried even harder." Which had him trying his best to comfort them, with zero success. He drew a deep breath, amazed at how glad he was to have her here with him again. Even when he knew it couldn't last. He wound up his story with a half grin. "And then you and Buttercup arrived and brought peace to the Rocking R once again."

"They are just overtired," she soothed. "And change can be hard on anyone."

He still felt like he was suddenly failing them, in a way he never had before. His frustration rose. "Yet you handle it."

"As do you." Emma briefly covered his hand with her own, her skin feeling warm and inviting against his. She squeezed his fingers before she let go and sat back, promising, "And your boys will, too."

He hoped she was right about that. Otherwise, it was going to be a very long twelve days until his mom returned from her trip. Aware how much he already owed her, he paused to let his gaze rove her face. "Thank you for coming over tonight."

She blushed prettily and kept her eyes on his. "You're welcome."

Leery of becoming a burden to her, he said, "But you don't have to come back for breakfast in the morning."

Her chin lifted with the stubborn determination he knew so well. "I'm not planning to." She smiled. "Buttercup and I are staying the night."

Chapter Six

The part of Tom that was still wildly attracted to Emma wanted to whoop with joy and hug her close. But the other part of him, which was wary of ever depending on her again, was a lot more apprehensive. He didn't want to start leaning on her, only to have her take off again to satisfy her ambition. More importantly, he didn't want his boys to do the same. They were already mourning the temporary loss of their grandmother...

How would they feel if they started to count on her and then Emma got so busy chasing her professional dreams again, she disappeared, too? She had a design studio to finish putting together, and that meeting with the RTW Bridal buyer coming up. Not to mention, local residents, some with deep pocketbooks, wanting tours…and maybe lots of expensive handcrafted shoes and boots, too.

"I appreciate your kindness."

Her expression grew conflicted and the corners of her lips turned down. "But you don't want me and Buttercup here overnight," she guessed.

He caught the brief, wistful look in her eyes. "I feel like the boys and I are taking advantage of you."

Another silence fell between them, this one fraught with tension. "You can only do that if the emotions involved are one-sided." She pushed back her chair and stood, moving away from the table. "That's not true in our case. You and I are on exactly the same page."

He followed her to the big bay windows, overlooking the backyard. "Which is…?"

"We want your mother to stay in Italy and enjoy her tour." She released an exasperated breath. "We want to be friends again, but we don't want it to go any further."

Right. Wait! Was that really true?

There was only one way to find out.

He kept his eyes on hers a disconcertingly long time. "So you're saying you don't desire me…" He stepped toward her.

She defiantly held her place, just as he suspected she would. Lifted her chin. "No. I actually do still feel the sparks."

As did he. More than ever.

He watched as she drew a deep breath, the action lifting the enticing curves of her soft breasts. "The difference is, I'm smarter this time around and I think you are, too."

Disappointment warred with his need to kiss her again. He eased back. "In what sense?"

"That we know what our futures hold. You're going to be here in Laramie County, and I'll be—" she gestured, not knowing "—wherever my career takes me."

For a long moment, Tom remained motionless. Silent. Leaving Emma to wonder—had she made a mistake? Been too honest? There was no one way to tell from the inscrutable expression on his maddeningly handsome face.

Finally, he relaxed. "You're right." His lips curved into the gently matter-of-fact smile she loved. "There is no need to borrow trouble."

And sex between us would be just that, Emma thought. Because it would make her want to turn back time, find a way to avoid the heartache that had torn them apart.

"We just have to get through the next few days, while the boys get acclimated to doing without my mom," Tom said.

She looked up at him. "Exactly."

"And if you can provide a feminine presence, and/or distraction that helps them cope, then—" he shrugged his wide shoulders affably "—I'd be a fool to turn you down."

His low masculine voice sent a thrill through her. Emma struggled to contain her pulse. "Not that your mother would let you."

Stepping away from her, Tom lounged against the counter, legs crossed at the ankles, hands braced on either side of him. "No. She has her own level of difficulty."

They smiled.

"Seriously," she said, as her entire body leaped into flame and he hadn't even made another move on her yet, "we both owe your mother. Me, for all the encouragement and support she gave me when I was trying to find the courage to pursue big, bold dreams. And you, for all the help she has provided you and your family."

Tom nodded. "I guess the only question remaining is, guest room or sofa?" He aimed a thumb at the center of his broad chest. "And you know where I think you should sleep."

The thought of being just down the hall from him was far too enticing. Her fantasies were going wild as it was. She shook her head, determined to stay firmly planted in the plain of reality. "Nope."

His chuckle was warm and seductive. "Why not? That living room couch can't be anywhere near as comfortable as the guest bed."

Pretending she couldn't feel the sizzle of awareness sifting through them, she backed up. "It's just fine. And for a lot of reasons, Buttercup and I prefer to be on the first floor. While you-all sleep upstairs."

His gaze evocatively traced the shape of her lips before returning to her eyes. "Fair enough."

He flashed another thoughtful half smile, then went upstairs to get the pillow and blankets, while she took Buttercup out one last time. And then, thankfully, there was nothing else to do but say good-night.

Tom walked into the kitchen early the next morning, looking rested and relaxed. But his dark brow furrowed when he stared at the breakfast items Emma had already laid out. "You've got to be kidding me," he said in that low, husky voice that melted her from the inside out.

She forced herself to continue the breakfast prep. "And here I thought you were a cowboy," she teased.

Tom's gaze drifted over her as he came even closer. His golden brown eyes darkened appreciatively as he took in her sleep-rumpled clothes from yesterday, her upswept hair, and makeup-free face. Unable to go through her usual morning routine, she felt at a distinct disadvantage. Yet all he seemed to be thinking as his eyes tracked back to the clip in her hair again, was hauling her close and taking her hair down.

Something he had done a lot when they'd been together and made love.

It had turned her on. Every. Single. Time.

She caught her breath at the relentless sensual intent in his gaze.

"Actually, I am a damn fine rancher," he drawled.

Who smelled incredibly good just out of the shower, Emma thought. Like brisk, woodsy cologne and the masculine soap he favored.

Finding she suddenly needed her physical space, she slanted him another playful look and continued setting the table for five. "Then you must know the first thing you do when you fall off a horse, is get right back on."

The room seemed to go completely still. He tensed but his expression did not change. "The boys are not going to like this."

She gestured magnanimously. "Yeah, well, that may be true, initially anyway, but they also need to broaden their horizons. Experience the 'bachelor' aka 'college dorm' lifestyle."

He nodded, beginning to understand. Chuckling, he said, "Keggers?"

Glad to see his sense of humor returning, Emma wrinkled her nose at him. "Ha-ha. No. I meant, fending for themselves, and helping you to do so, too. They need to know they don't always need a woman in their lives to take care of them to feel safe and happy."

Tom tilted his head. "But it sure can be nice sometimes…" he volleyed back.

Emma flushed, not sure what that meant.

Before she could pursue his line of thought, the boys came dashing through the downstairs. Their footsteps stopped at the sofa, then they turned and headed for the kitchen.

"You're awake!" Crockett announced.

"We thought you were going to be sleeping like a princess!" Bowie said.

"Yeah, and you would need a prince to wake you up," Austin concluded.

Tom winked at Emma. "No kissing princes here."

Was that really true? she wondered silently. To the triplets, she said, "It's a good thing Buttercup and I are already awake." This way, she wouldn't have to worry about any further romantic missteps.

Abruptly, all three boys frowned.

"What is that?" Crockett looked at the box of frozen waffles.

"We had that last night!" Bowie complained.

"And we did not like it," Austin lamented with a sad little pout.

Emma focused on the budding rebellion. Using the skill she had amassed taking care of all of her nieces and nephews, she told the boys cheerfully, "Well, that is because your daddy did it all wrong!"

Not surprisingly, they agreed with her there.

"And I am here to teach him how to do it all right."

Crockett edged closer, looking interested despite himself. "Why don't you just make them regular?"

"With the machine" Bowie pointed to the waffle iron. "And the mixing bowl and stuff."

"Because we don't always have time for that," Emma explained. "Of course," she added, sighing dramatically and putting on a sad little pout herself, "if you boys think that I don't know how to make these taste really, really good, either...then..." She forced herself to look even sadder.

Austin came closer and tucked his hand in hers. "We'll help you try, Miss Emma."

There was no feigning her delight. "Really?" She beamed down at all three of them.

They nodded in agreement. "But if it doesn't work," Crockett warned, "I'm eating cereal."

* * *

The trick with frozen waffles, Tom learned, was putting them through the toaster twice on a medium light setting. That way they stayed nice and golden and crunchy on the outside, but soft and warm on the inside. Adding more variety of toppings—everything from warmed fruit spread and/or syrup to softened butter mixed with cinnamon sugar—enhanced the excitement, as did letting the boys "make it snow" on their plate with powdered sugar. And even add dollops of whipped cream.

They were so happy, in fact, they all had seconds. Which, he figured, made up for the culinary catastrophe of the night before.

They were just getting up from the table when the phone rang. It was his mom.

Tom accepted the FaceTime request, and turned the phone so she could see all three of the boys looking happy and content. "Hi, Gramma," Austin said.

"Miss Emma taught Daddy how to make waffles," Bowie reported.

"They were good this time," Crockett added.

A big smile lit up their grandmother's face. "Well, that's wonderful!" she said.

The boys chattered on, telling her how much fun they were having playing with Buttercup. The call ended with Marjorie relieved and happy again.

That did not mean, however, that his sons wanted to go to school. Luckily, all it took to change their minds was a promise from Emma that they could stop by her place afterward and tell her all about it.

Thank you, Tom mouthed over the kids' heads.

"No problem," she murmured back, with a sweet maternal smile that stayed with Tom long after he had dropped his kids off at preschool. And gone back to the Rocking R to talk to his foreman and the hired hands about the work that needed to be done that week.

It was amazing how much Emma had done for him in only a few days. If she hadn't been there to help, his mother would already be plotting a way to cut her trip short. And he would have been up half the night with the kids and getting them to school this morning would have been hard as heck. But because she had sacrificed her time and energy to lend a hand, his family was doing a whole lot better.

He hadn't really shown his gratitude. It was high time he did.

Emma had just put out all the shoes and boots she needed to look at when the buzzer rang. Curious, because she wasn't expecting any deliveries, she pushed the intercom button. "Yes?"

"A surprise for Miss Emma Lockhart," a deep, familiar voice rumbled.

She paused. A glance at her watch showed it was a little past twelve noon. Which meant the kids were still in pre-K for almost another four hours. Or should be, anyway. She hoped nothing had happened! "Tom…?"

He chuckled in confirmation. "Yep."

Emma let out her breath, relieved that her ex didn't have that stressed note in his voice that presaged any crisis. Instead, he sounded happier than she had heard him since they had started crossing paths again. Wishing she hadn't just made such a mess of her living space, she hit the unlock button on the security panel. "Come on up."

The outer door opened and closed. Footsteps sounded on the stairs. She swung the apartment door wide and greeted him as he hit the landing just outside her unit, drink in one hand, bag from the Cowgirl Chef in the other. His glance roved over her, taking in the coil of hair on top of her head, still damp from the shower. As well as her oversize work shirt, cutoffs and sneakers. He grinned, clearly liking what he saw. She liked what she saw, too, and knew she shouldn't be this elated to see him, but she was.

"What do you have there?" she asked, her heart already racing in anticipation of time spent alone with him.

"Apple walnut chicken salad on a croissant, and a vanilla latte with an extra shot of espresso."

Pleased he had recalled her favorite midday meal, she stepped back to let him pass and ushered him in. "Wow. What's the occasion?"

Their fingertips brushed as he handed her the coffee and the bag. "I just wanted to say thank you for all your help the last week. First with my mom when she got hurt, and then the boys."

Tingling from the brief contact, she walked over to make space for her lunch on the dining table. "You're welcome."

As the moment drew out, she had the strongest sensation he wanted to kiss her. Worse, she wanted to kiss him, too. But they had promised themselves they wouldn't go there again, so she averted her gaze. And tried her darnedest to figure a polite way to send him on his merry way before things got out of hand.

"I'd offer you a seat, but everything is pretty much covered at the moment." Even the chairs from the table had been lined up in a row, their seats filled with sample shoes and boots. Ditto the sofa, wing chairs, floors, tops of travel trunks and end tables.

Bracing his hands on his waist, he took it all in with an admiring glance. Reminding her how much of a cheerleader he had been for her dreams before tragedy hit, inevitably forcing them apart.

"Did you make all these?" he asked.

She sipped her coffee. Delicious. "Over the last few years, yes."

He looked around again, clearly impressed. "How many different styles are there?"

"I have thirty different shoes, and twenty kinds of boots, but as you can see most of them are some variation of this." She held up the lace-up midcalf boot with the two-inch heel.

"You say that like it's a problem."

She cleared the seats of two wing chairs and gestured for him to take a seat while she piled the samples on top of one of the wheeled travel trunks she took to shows. "I didn't think it was going to be since initially the buyer from Ready To Wear Bridal shops was only interested in seeing the different versions of my wedding boot. But then, I got an email a little while ago, letting me know that she had changed her mind after talking to their CEO and wanted to see anything and everything that might possibly work with a wedding gown."

He studied her intently. "And that's not good?"

With a sigh, she removed the sandwich from its plastic container. "I don't want to give up too much of my intellectual property before I know how well things are going to work out." She took a bite and found the sandwich to be as tasty as it appeared. Which was good because she was starving.

"Makes sense."

Not wanting to count her chickens before they hatched, Emma swallowed her second bite, then wiped the corners of her mouth with a napkin. "Assuming, of course, they will still be interested in doing business with me after they visit the design studio. Which—" she sighed again, picking up her coffee "—is far from a sure thing."

He regarded her with utter certainty. "Then don't."

She paused, midsip.

He approached so she had no choice but to look him in the eye. "Even I can see you are incredibly talented, and I don't know anything about ladies' footwear."

His support meant a lot. *Too much?*

Emma shrugged and moved away restlessly. Her appetite suddenly fading. She glanced at him over one shoulder. "I'm not sure at this point I can afford to be that picky. After already striking out twice. And yet, at the same time—" she surveyed her creations passionately "—these designs represent years of dedication and hard work. So, to give up on all that effort, and

cede total control, on just the promise of success…"
When she knew business deals fell through all the
time. Especially in the fashion world.

He closed the distance between them. "First of all,"
he murmured as he took her into his arms and pulled
her close, "this isn't baseball…"

"Good thing," she joked back as her heart began to
race. Their bodies touched in one long electric line.
When she tilted her face up to his, Tom's sexy grin
widened all the more. "Because otherwise I'd be on
the verge of being out," she remarked ruefully, com-
forted by how easy it was to confess her most private
insecurities to him. "And," she added, her voice turning unaccountably husky, "not necessarily just for one
inning…"

He gazed affectionately down at her, offering comfort as only he could. The pad of his thumb scored her
lower lip. "Trust me, Emma." He paused, tenderness
pushing aside the mischief in his eyes. "All your hard
work has not been for naught." He traced her cheek-
bone, too. "You've got this."

Did she?

Aware how long it had been since she had been
looked after by any man, never mind him, she opened
her mouth to speak. Before she could get a sound out,
he bent down, his lips hovering over hers. She knew
he was going to kiss her. Knew all the reasons why
she shouldn't let him. But her will to resist faded as he
brushed his mouth against hers. Subtly, languorously.

The softness of her breasts pressed into the wall of
his chest. Lower still, she found she was just as mal-

leable. And just that swiftly, the testing contact turned into something else. She caught her breath as the ache rose in her throat. "Tom…"

He drew her closer yet. His hands slid down her spine, flattening her against him. Seducing her deep into his embrace. "I know." He kissed her again, his lips hot and supple, wickedly sensual and possessive. "We talked about this." And still he kissed her, his tongue exploring her mouth, laying claim to her inner recesses, again and again, until her toes curled, her knees weakened. Passion swept through her and she released a small moan of both pleasure and of the need to be closer.

He broke off the kiss and reached up to undo the clip in her hair, letting the strands fall loose about her shoulders. He stroked his fingers through the silken strands, luxuriating in the feel of her hair. The way he had in the past.

And just that quickly, the make-out session turned into something else. Something deeper, more meaningful.

She looked into his eyes. He looked into hers.

Then he cupped her face in his big, strong hands. "I know this could screw everything up, if it were to all go south, make us enemies again." He shook his head, sweet and tender yearning encompassing his low voice. "But damn, Emma, I have missed you so much."

Being with him like this made her want to do something for herself. Instead of just everyone else. It made her want to focus on something other than work. Ambition. Money and fame.

He made her want to give in to the moment, just for a little while. She arched against him, wanting and needing him so much. Savoring the proof of his desire. "I missed you, too," she whispered back.

And though love and permanence weren't exactly in the equation, a feeling of rightness swept through her, intensifying the sweet yearning she felt deep inside.

He delivered another kiss. Then another. And another. Until his hand stilled on her waist. He rested his forehead on hers, his ragged breathing echoing the meter of her own. "Tell me to go..."

That's all it would take. She knew. She shook her head, still holding him so close they were almost one. "Later..." she murmured against his mouth. And then taking him by the hand, she led him toward her bedroom.

Tom knew he was going to make love to Emma again, before all was said and done. There was too much history, too much unfinished business and pent-up emotion simmering between them for it not to happen. He was pretty certain that she knew it, too.

He just hadn't figured it would be *today*.

He didn't think she had expected this, either. And that brought up a big yellow caution sign. They had hurt each other enough in the past. He had to make certain this was not going to be something she would later regret. "Sure about this?" he asked.

Regarding him boldly, she slipped off her shirt, then her jeans. Her entire body softening in surrender, she reached for the buttons on his shirt. "Very..."

The queen-size brass bed was the same one she'd had in her apartment, her senior year of college. The linens were different. More sophisticated than feminine and frilly. But it was as comfortable as ever, he discovered, as they stretched out between the sheets.

It had been ages since he had been able to kiss her like this or felt the soft swell of her breasts nestled against his chest. And it had definitely been too long since he had seen her naked. His whole body tightened as he rubbed his thumbs across the tender crests of her breasts. Felt her impatience and heard her moan, soft and low in her throat.

Eager to please her, he shifted her onto her back and slid down between her thighs. He kissed his way across her breasts and belly. Caught her hips with his hands and went lower still.

"Oh, Tom…" she whispered, quivering and arching her back.

When she would have hurried, he held back. "We've got time…to do this right…" he murmured, stroking and kissing her hot, satiny skin. The delicate folds. "Let me…"

Closing her eyes and fisting her hands in his hair, she sighed tremulously and gave herself over to him. His spirits rising, he savored her sweet femininity, the way she opened herself up to the moment and the passion they shared.

Perspiration beaded her body; the insides of her thighs were lined with moisture. He suckled the silky nub and stroked inside her. Until her thighs fell even farther apart.

"Now," she whimpered, quaking with need.

He paused to find protection, then easing his hands beneath her, he lifted her. She wrapped her arms and legs around him, clasping him close, taking him into her, giving him everything he wanted and needed. She was all woman as she arched up to meet him, her response as uninhibited as he hoped it would be. He plunged and withdrew, aware of every soft, yielding inch of her, every moan, every sigh, every shudder of need and yearning. At once, achingly familiar and thrillingly brand-new.

Emma had been his first love. For many, many years his only love. And now that he was finally making love to her again, Tom thought, as they clung together, free-falling into sweet oblivion, he never wanted to let her go.

Chapter Seven

Aftershocks surged through Emma's body, giving her a cozy satisfaction she hadn't felt in years. She lay on her back, forearm drawn across her eyes, doing her best to catch her breath. And stop wishing they could make love all over again.

Tom misunderstood her silence. "So this is where the regrets come in," he drawled.

A self-conscious flush started in her chest and moved into her face. He had already underestimated her at the worst times. She wasn't going to let him do it again. "No." She sat up, dragging the sheet with her, and shoved a hand through her hair. "No regrets." As much as the vulnerable side of her would have liked to avoid hooking up again to protect her heart, she knew that this had probably been inevitable... "I think this had to happen…so we would not be left wondering if the sparks were truly still there."

"And were they?" Tom asked.

Emma let her gaze drift over his big, powerful frame. All that smooth satiny skin… The thing about being in love with someone for years, and having them love you back, was that even after you broke up, a certain depth of intimacy remained.

She elbowed him lightly in the side, appreciating how handsome and sexy he looked, lounging in her bed. "I think you know they were," she said dryly. "For both of us."

"But…?"

She wished he would quit fueling romantic fantasies that had too long gone unexplored. She rose, snatching up her clothes with fingers that trembled slightly. "Our chemistry doesn't necessarily make this a good idea."

Languidly, he rose, too. Making no effort to hide his nakedness. Or the fact he was still aroused. "What would?"

She slipped into the bathroom, and with the door only slightly ajar, began to dress. "At this point?" She spoke through the opening, reality descending with crushing force. "Knowing where we both are in our lives?" *The fact I will most likely be leaving again in six months?* "Probably nothing."

She strolled back out, just in time to see him zip up his jeans and pull on his shirt. He left it open and drew her back into the cradle of his arms. "I understand what you are saying, sweetheart." He stroked a hand through her hair. "And I would agree. If there were strings attached to what just happened. But…if there aren't…"

Emma locked her gaze on his, already feeling her carefully built defenses falling. He was who he was, take it or leave it. She was the same way. She tried not to think how much that gave them in common.

She ignored the low insistent quiver in her belly. "You're saying you want a no-strings relationship?"

He tucked her hair behind her ear, kissed her temple. Then gave her that look that let her know he was much more complex, deep down, than he often let on. He lifted his wide shoulders in a careless shrug. "Why not?" he countered, still holding her eyes.

Because if I spend too much time in your arms, I might fall in love with you all over again. And she wasn't sure her tender heart could stand that. Especially if he let her go this time, as readily as he had the last, when their goals diverged.

She stepped outside the circle of his arms. "Because sex makes things complicated, Tom. With or without love."

He delivered a slow, heart-stopping smile. "*People* make things complicated. And we already established neither of us wants that right now. Our individual lives are crazy enough. Without us trying to permanently merge two very different sets of life expectations."

Was she crazy? Why was he suddenly making complete sense? She had never been the kind of woman who could indulge in one-night stands or be bed buddies with someone she found physically attractive. Or do without emotional commitment.

Yet, here she was, entertaining the idea of a friends-with-benefits arrangement with the one and only love of her life.

As always, Tom could sense when he was breaking down her defenses. "You don't have to decide now," he told her. And she knew from his patient, understanding regard, he meant it. He would wait as long as she required.

Another point in his favor. Her pulse still skittering, she flashed a half smile, said softly, "Thank you for that."

His eyes were dark and unwavering on hers. "Just tell me you'll think about it," he said in the low, husky voice she loved.

She trembled at the raw tenderness on his face. "I will."

He started to head for the door, then stopped, looked around. She knew he was noticing the same thing she was. In the bright midday sunlight, the walls she had refused to get painted prior to move in, looked dingier than ever. The paint was fading in places, grungy in others. She had tried washing the worst places yet somehow the dirt had remained.

Tom shook his head. "I don't know how you stand this. You really should let me get this repainted for you."

Waving off his offer, she said, "I don't want workers underfoot right now." It would be too distracting. Probably noisy, too.

He trod closer, towering over her. "Then I'll do it."

Even worse. Then she really wouldn't be able to

concentrate! Especially after today! Just the thought of him so close and undeniably sexy was enough to bathe her in the heat of desire, head to toe.

She propped her hands on her hips. "Don't you have ranch chores to do and cattle to look after?"

"My foreman and hired hands are taking care of ninety-nine percent of it while my mother is away."

Made sense. Especially given how much of a full-time job his three preschoolers had been the last few days.

Tom examined a small dent in the drywall, which needed patched, too. "If you choose a color, I could knock this out in two days while the boys are in pre-K."

The image of him painting was more than she could take. She did not need to see those powerful muscles of his flex, again and again, as he worked. Though, for some reason, her heart fluttered wildly at the thought. "Thanks, but…"

As he continued to look around, in full landlord mode now, his eyes fell on the kitchen sink. A big drop gathered beneath the end of the old-fashioned spigot, then splattered onto the porcelain below.

Frowning, he walked over to examine it. "How long has that been dripping?"

"Um. I don't know. I really haven't noticed."

His brow lifted.

Clearly, he wasn't buying her fib. "Okay, okay. Since shortly after I moved in," she confessed. "But it only drips once every fifteen minutes or so."

"I really need to replace the whole thing."

She wasn't arguing that. She still didn't want him underfoot until after her big meeting with RTW Bridal. Especially since it really wasn't an emergency. She had lived in a much worse place in Philadelphia, during grad school.

She picked up the latte he had given her, found it had gone cold. "Did the fixtures you special ordered for it come in?" She debated whether to gently heat the coffee in the microwave or add ice.

"No, but like I told you before... I can put in builder grade temporarily, and then replace it with the nicer stuff when it does come in—" he checked his phone for the information "—at the end of next week."

Her frustration grew. She really did not need him going Sir Galahad on her. If he had let his former tenant, the surgical resident, forego any upgrades to the apartment so he could sleep whenever he had the chance, why couldn't he let her forego them so she could work nonstop? "That sounds like a lot of unnecessary trouble."

The grooves on either side of his mouth deepened. "Unless it fails entirely..."

Deciding she didn't want the rest of the latte after all, she set it back down and swung back to him. "What are you talking about?"

He strode over to the faucet. "This is ancient. Has it been giving you any other issues?"

"Like what?"

"Like not wanting to turn on or shut off."

Uh-oh. Was that a bad sign, too? "Well, I mean, it's a little finicky, but it still works, and if the new stuff is coming in at the end of next week, and I don't use it a lot between now and then, it should be just fine."

His broad shoulders relaxed. He finally saw her reasoning, she thought with a wave of relief. But then he turned back toward her, giving her an intent look. "You'll tell me if it gets worse?"

She held up her palm as if taking the oath of office. "I promise you will be the first person I call, Wheeler-Dealer Cowboy Tom."

"All right, Princess Lady Emma." He gestured at the kitchen sink and dingy walls, the outdated appliances that while still working, really did seem to be on their last legs. "I'll let you have your way. For now. I just hope all of this *stays* at nuisance level." On that note of warning, he strode out.

At four fifteen that afternoon, the Reid triplets came over after school, as promised, and walked into Emma's work studio.

"We got homework," Crockett announced.

"But Daddy says it is all the same," Bowie explained.

"Even though we got different teachers now," Austin announced, matter-of-fact.

"We don't have to talk about that now," Tom said gently.

"'Cause we got a whole week to do it," Crockett said.

Wow, Emma thought. Must be some project.

"And we're here for another reason," their dad continued.

"Cookies?" Emma quipped, bringing out the individual boxes of animal crackers and juice boxes she had for them.

The boys grinned, accepting the gift with a unified thank-you, and looked around for a place to sit. Finally settling down on a long leather-seated bench that would eventually go in the retail space.

"We want to invite you and Buttercup for dinner," Tom explained.

"Oh yeah? When and where?" Emma handed him a bottle of iced tea.

"Where we all live. The Rocking R ranch," Crockett said.

"Tonight, when you're done with work, but before our bedtime," Bowie added.

Austin smiled shyly. "Us and Daddy are going to make it real special!"

"Well, that does sound wonderful," Emma said, smiling down at the boys.

"Six o'clock okay with you?" Tom asked.

Noting how quickly the triplets were getting used to being under the sole care of their dad, not to mention how often they were seeking out her company, she said, "Perfect."

Maybe she wasn't a mom yet. But she could still enjoy spending time with kids. And Tom's boys were very sweet indeed.

"Look, Daddy, Miss Emma is coming!"

"She sure is." He watched her get out of her SUV and help Buttercup down to the ground.

She looked gorgeous in a pair of jeans and cowgirl

boots, an open-throated calico shirt—the same color as the bluebonnets in the field—with her hair loose and free around her shoulders.

His pulse leaped as she moved toward them. Tipping her cowgirl hat at them as she neared.

The boys broke out into wide grins. Indicating he wasn't the only one who was getting attached. And though he would have worried about that a week before, now, well…he found himself trusting in fate, the way he hadn't since he and Emma had broken up.

Maybe all this was a sign. That they were meant to be in each other's lives.

Oblivious to the hopeful nature of his thoughts, she bounded up the steps onto the covered front porch, where a table had been set with care. "Wow, guys," she said, pointing at the mason jars of wildflowers, and the hurricane lanterns with candles. "This is beautiful! I am impressed!"

"Wait till you eat what we fixed," Austin said proudly.

"They did the menu all by themselves," Tom explained.

"But Daddy helped us fix stuff," Crockett cut in.

"Ready to help bring it all out, fellas?" Tom asked.

The boys eagerly headed for the door. "You sit down, Miss Emma," Bowie said.

"But don't worry, we got something for Buttercup, too!"

Emma's eyes lit up. "We really are getting the red carpet treatment!" She sat at the place designated for her. Glad she had always been such a good sport, Tom shepherded his crew inside the house where a lot of commotion ensued.

Eventually, he had everyone organized, and the boys came back out, carefully carrying their plastic containers of food. He managed the only hot dish. The repast included English muffin cheese pizzas, celery sticks spread with cream cheese and dotted with raisins, clementines and messily put together peanut butter crackers.

Emma had leashed Buttercup to the railing, so they wouldn't have to worry about her running off. Tom brought her a small bowl of food, and another dish of water. "It's the same kibble you've been feeding her."

"Thank you. That is so sweet. In fact, guys, this whole dinner looks absolutely incredible."

She regarded them all with maternal grace, alerting him what a good mother she would make someday.

The boys were very serious, their little chests puffed out importantly, as they passed around the dishes, helping themselves and offering to assist Emma, as well. As they all dug in, the triplets explained in great detail how every dish had been first decided upon, and then prepared.

Emma beamed at Austin, Bowie and Crockett as they talked animatedly, her gentle presence feeling like a port in the storm. It reinforced for Tom how much he had missed having her in his life.

"The whole meal was glorious," she said, putting her napkin aside when the last bite had been eaten. She smiled at his sons. "Do you all want to play with

Buttercup in the backyard for a minute while I help your dad with the cleanup?"

"Yes!" they shouted in unison.

"Thanks for being such a good sport," he murmured, noticing all over again how damn pretty she looked. How sweet and feminine she smelled.

Looking like she wanted to kiss him again as much as he wanted to kiss her, she said, "Thanks for having me."

The boys dashed back in, Buttercup trotting alongside them. Crockett peered at Emma intently. "Are you going to sleep on the sofa again tonight?"

For the first time all evening, she tensed. "Actually, I was thinking Buttercup and I might head back to town tonight." Three little faces fell. "Because I do have a lot of work to do at my studio," she added.

"But I was thinking, maybe if you all got up a little early tomorrow morning, and were extra good listeners for your daddy, that you all could meet me before school and we could all have a special breakfast together. What do you think about that?"

A contemplative silence fell.

It wasn't what they had been hoping for. Him, either, Tom realized in surprise.

"Would you at least tuck us in?" Crockett asked finally.

"And read us bedtime stories?" Bowie said.

"And stay until we go to sleep?" Austin added.

Emma looked at Tom for a decision.

Luckily, she seemed to realize, as did he, they were on the verge of another meltdown.

He gave her a look, beseeching her to stay just a while longer.

"Of course," she said, flashing a sweet smile.

While Tom supervised, the boys brushed their teeth, bathed and put their pajamas on. Finished, they raced down the stairs to get Emma and Tom was right behind them. As they moved in tandem, he realized, they could all get used to this.

Chapter Eight

Emma hadn't been on the second floor of the Rocking R ranch house in years.

Not a lot had changed.

Tom occupied one en suite bedroom, Marjorie the other. The guest room was located next to his, and the other two bedrooms were for the boys. One was a playroom with a big chenille rug, and plenty of room to build things and drive their toy cars and trucks around. The other was a sleep space for all three.

Crockett, who had been excitedly leading the way, tugged on Emma's hand. "Do you like our room?" He pulled her inside.

Emma looked over the cozy rug, navy blue walls and crisp white trim. The three beds were lined up, side by side, and covered with coordinating but dif-

ferent red, white and blue bed linens. THE ALPHA-
BET GANG had been stenciled on the wall above,
with their names painted in the same pretty script on
the headboards of their beds. A small table, lamp and
framed photograph sat next to each bed. And to round
out the decor, a rocker-glider sat in the corner, facing
the beds, a basket of storybooks beside it.

"This is super awesome!" she exclaimed.

Austin took her other hand and guided her over to
the rocker. "You sit here," he informed her. "See that?"
He pointed to THE ALPHABET GANG painted on the
wall. "That's our *nickname*," he told her importantly.

"And it's a very good one," Emma agreed, aware
she seemed to be taking Tom's seat. However, he didn't
appear to mind, and she felt even more included in
their family life. A wave of almost maternal satisfaction ebbed through her, as Crockett edged close. "Do
you have a nickname?" he asked.

Tom caught Emma's eyes, letting her know she did
not have to reveal that if she did not choose to. But she
didn't mind them knowing. She smiled at them, taking in their cute little faces. "Yes, I do."

"What is it?" Austin asked, sitting partway on her
lap.

"Princess Lady Emma."

"Wow! That's a cool name," Bowie declared.

His brothers nodded enthusiastically. "Did Daddy
have a nickname when he was a kid?" Crockett asked,
intuiting correctly that she would know the answer
to that.

"Yes, he did." Emma smiled at their dad.

He made a gesture that seemed to say, *Go ahead, I have it coming.*

"What was it?" Austin asked.

"Wheeler-Dealer Cowboy Tom."

Bowie comically scrunched up his face. "What's that mean?"

"Well," Emma began, "a wheeler-dealer is a person who likes to be in the center of the action and likes to win at whatever is going on." Which still seemed true today, she thought, flashing Tom a look. "And of course, we all know what a cowboy is."

"Oh." The boys contemplated.

"Can we call you Princess Lady Emma?" Bowie asked. "Instead of Miss Emma?"

Aware it had a certain charm to it, she smiled. It would also have the added bonus of taking something that had irritated her in the past, and make it something sweet that she looked forward to hearing. From The Alphabet Gang, anyway.

She hugged them all reassuringly. "Sure. I think I would like that."

They hugged her back.

"But we're still going to call Daddy… *Daddy*," Austin declared, speaking for all three. Bowie and Crockett nodded. "'Cause we like that better."

Tom glanced at his watch and headed toward her, as if ready to take over. "Okay, fellas. Time for your bedtime story. Tomorrow is a school day, you know."

Crockett and Austin blocked his path while Bowie rifled through the wicker basket, pulled out a book and handed it to Emma instead. "You can read this one to us tonight," he said.

The boys dashed to climb beneath their covers. Hands folded behind their heads, they prepared to listen while Tom eased back to lounge in the doorway once again, giving her wordless permission to proceed.

A little self-consciously, Emma began. But was soon caught up in the story of a garbage truck that worked all night, picking up trash all over the city, and taking it to the recycling center. Only to go to sleep again at dawn when the rest of the city was waking up.

The boys smiled as she finished.

Tom guided them through their prayers, which included a wish that Marjorie would return home soon, and blessings for Tom, a number of their pre-K friends and Emma and Buttercup, too.

Then the boys turned, and pressing two fingers to their lips, tenderly transferred a kiss to the framed photo beside their bed. "Night, Momma," they said.

Caught off guard by the sweet sentimentality of the moment, Emma found herself blinking back tears as the boys turned back to her and Tom. "Hug, Daddy!" they said.

Tom complied.

"Princess Lady Emma!" It was more of a command than a request.

Emma gathered them close one by one, loving the affection they gave so freely and breathing in their sweet little boy scent.

She had always known, deep down, she wanted children. But tonight, the fact she had none of her own, was an ache deep in her heart that reverberated long after she said good-night.

"Thanks for humoring the guys tonight," Tom said, as they headed downstairs.

Aware this memory would stick with her, along with all the rest of the time she spent with Tom and his children, she exhaled. "My pleasure."

He fell into step beside her, as they reached the first floor, and walked with her through the spacious downstairs of the ranch house. "Not everyone would be so generous with their time and attention."

A blissful silence fell. Emma searched out her dog, who was still sleeping on the folded blanket that he had set up for her in a corner of his kitchen. "I wouldn't bet on that. They're really cute little kiddos."

Buttercup stretched and stood. Then went straight to the back door and turned to look at them. Signaling she needed to go out.

Tom switched on the outdoor lights. They followed the dog outside and stood on the patio as dusk turned to dark. The spring air was warm and slightly breezy, and the scent of Marjorie's flowers perfumed the air. Making it a perfect night for kissing. But that couldn't happen again, Emma reminded herself sternly. Not if she wanted to keep her heart intact. So, as Buttercup nosed her way around the backyard, she remarked casually, "I liked their bedroom a lot, too."

He looked her in the eye, protective and take charge in the way she had always yearned for a man to be. "Vicki did all that."

The husky timbre of his voice sent a thrill up and down her spine.

Emma edged several inches away. She did not know much about his late wife. Mostly, because she hadn't wanted to learn. Now, seeing how the boys related to their mother, she wanted to know more about the obviously loving and caring woman who had given birth to them. "She came up with the idea for The Alphabet Gang, too?"

Tom's lips curved upward, as he reflected. "As well as their first names. She was a middle school Texas history teacher when I met her. When we found out we were having all boys, she wanted to name them after three of her favorite historical figures."

Ah. Now it all made sense. "Stephen F. Austin, James Bowie and Davy Crockett."

"Right. We figured if we had any more kids—she wanted three girls, too—that we would keep going through the alphabet."

Emma imagined the Rocking R filled with kids. And the happily married couple who had given birth to them. "That would've been a big family."

He shrugged one broad shoulder affably. He looked so handsome in the fading light, it was all she could do not to snuggle in his arms. "I always admired yours. How close you and your siblings were. Whereas I was an only child." He moved closer once again. "That could get kind of lonely."

Her heart skittered in her chest. "I guess so."

And speaking of missing out when it came to family... She sobered, recalling the most emotional moment of the evening. So far, anyway. "The photos of their mom, and themselves as babies, next to the bed seem to really comfort them. Were they always there?"

He took her hand in his and led her over to the glider. "No." He sat down beside her, his jeans-clad thigh nudging hers, but did not let go of her palm. "That started after Vicki passed. The boys were only two. They couldn't understand why their mommy wasn't there to tuck them in anymore. I kept explaining to them that she was in heaven, but they still thought she would be coming back. So, finally, I put up the photos and started having them 'tell Mommy' whatever they wanted her to know, every night before they said their prayers and went to sleep. They wanted to blow her a kiss, too, the way they used to when she was alive." Tom's voice cracked slightly, and he withdrew his hand from hers. Ran it down his thigh. His voice became even rustier when he spoke again. "So that became a tradition, too."

Emma's eyes filled with tears.

"Oh, Tom. I'm so sorry for your loss." Not knowing what what else to do—she had been living in Italy at the time Vicki passed—she turned and gave him the consoling hug she would have bestowed on him at the funeral. Had she been here to attend. He returned the embrace the way he would have then, too. As if by rote.

He pulled back, his features taut with grief. "You really loved her, didn't you?" Emma said softly.

He nodded, his expression closed.

She was glad about that. A person could never have too much love or family in their life. And she hadn't been here, so…there really was no reason to be jealous, and she wasn't.

A little sad maybe, for all she had missed out on, had she stayed and married him herself, but she was not envious or resentful… How could she be when his marriage to Vicki had given him three such wonderful little boys? And made him into the generous man he was today?

Finished, Buttercup trotted toward them.

They rose and walked across the patio, opening the door to let Buttercup back inside.

Wordlessly, Tom bypassed the kitchen and mudroom and led her toward the addition at the rear of the home, behind the garage. The large room had once been his dad's study and ranch office. Now, clearly, it was Tom's abode.

She looked around, reacquainting herself with the stone fireplace. Beamed ceilings. Built-in bookcases. Heavy leather furniture. He walked over to the bar and poured himself a scotch.

Emma shook her head, declining one for herself.

"Is that why you've apparently decided that you will never marry again?" she asked.

He paused, glass halfway to his mouth. "How do you know that?"

Because you said, "Marriage is a lot of work!" Implying too much work for now. With effort, she ignored the sexual tension suddenly simmering between them. Focusing on what they could discuss. "Please. You're a very good-looking, very eligible bachelor with three adorable boys who need a mother. Every single woman in Laramie County who wants a family has secretly wondered *what-if...?*"

He chuckled, his eyes holding hers for a long moment. "Does that include you?"

Ignoring the tautening of her nipples, she replied sweetly, "I never said I wanted a family." Although she had privately wished for it many, many times.

"Your maternal instincts say you do."

Reaction shimmered through her, along with a deep-seated need that had gone too many years without sating.

Emma pushed the yearning aside. Reminding herself that she couldn't afford to get involved with a man who was still not 100 percent over the loss of his late spouse. "Back to Vicki... How did the two of you meet?"

Tom drained his glass, set it aside. "At a mutual friend's wedding." He inhaled sharply and ran a hand through his hair. "She was having a rough time because she was an only child like me and had just lost her own parents in an accident." He moved over to the fireplace, and stood looking at framed family photos there.

Sorrow etched his low, matter-of-fact tone. "My dad had passed a year or so before, so I was a little further along in the grieving process than she was, but I empathized the way only someone else who has been through that can. And we started talking." He paced, looking out at the dark spring night. "One thing led to another, and I went home with her that night. Six months later, we got married, and she got pregnant right away."

"I'm guessing she was a very good wife and mother."

"Yeah." Tom pressed the heels of his hands over his eyes. His shoulders sagged. "I just wish I'd been as good a husband."

His regret was palpable. Emma edged closer. "What are you talking about?"

He dropped his palms and looked over at her, admitting gruffly, "If I hadn't failed her so badly, she might be alive today."

The second the words were out, Tom regretted them. Too late. Emma had heard, and he knew she was not the type of woman who would ever let a confession like that go.

She stared at him, the soft corners of her lips turning down. "I find that hard to believe."

Guilt reignited. "Believe it," he bit out.

Emma squinted, as if struggling to recall what she had heard. "I thought Vicki was ill…"

"She was." Tom frowned, his misery deepening. "The problem was that none of us realized it. We all thought her fatigue and the weight loss was due to chasing after eighteen-month old triplets all day long." He scrubbed a hand over his face and began to pace again, confessing his own part in the tragedy. "I mean, my mom lived with us, and she did a lot, too, but I was out on the ranch all day, so by the time I got in at night, I barely had time to help with their supper, and baths, and get them in bed. By then, all Vicki wanted to do was collapse, so a lot of the time, I told her to go on to bed and get as much sleep as she could."

"Did that help?"

"Yes and no. She said she felt better but she kept losing weight, and there were days when she was so pale." He shook his head in frustration, remembering. "I asked her to go to the doctor for a checkup but she kept putting it off. Or so I thought."

Emma's hand covered her heart, even as she held his gaze. "Please tell me she didn't go and then not tell you what she found out."

Unfortunately, that was exactly what had happened. "Vicki didn't want anyone to know she had stage four pancreatic cancer."

She gasped. "Why not?" Compassion shone in her emerald green eyes.

"She knew everyone would try and talk her into doing chemotherapy to extend her life. And she didn't want to do it."

Emma closed the distance between them and took his hand. Gently, she led him over to the sofa to sit down, settling beside him. "Then how did you find out, if she didn't tell you?"

Tom leaned into the warmth of her touch. "She collapsed one day and ended up in the ER." His gut ached, remembering that horrible day. "No one said anything to me directly, but I could tell something was going on, and I eventually got it out of her."

Emma searched his face. Seeming to know instinctively what a mess he had been, at least on the inside.

Outwardly, he'd been as strong and stoic as his family had needed him to be. "How did you react?"

"My emotions were all over the place. I was angry. At Vicki, for not telling me, at God for letting this happen. I wanted her in the most aggressive treatment. ASAP. But she wouldn't hear of it. Her cancer had metastasized. With or without chemo, she only had a matter of months to live, and she didn't want to spend it away from me and her three little guys. She didn't want their last memories of her to be of her suffering the many side effects of chemo."

Tom fell silent. Reflecting on that awful time.

"It took a while, with me talking to a lot of different doctors about options, but eventually I saw her point. She wanted quality of life to the very end, not quantity, most of which would be spent in hospice.

"So I hired people to help with the ranch, and spent every last day here at the house with her and the boys."

He swallowed around the growing lump in his throat. "She passed about two months after that."

Tears were sliding down Emma's face. She gripped his hands harder. "Were you able to be with her in her final moments?"

"Yes. I was holding her hand. The boys came in, too, but she was unconscious, and they thought she was sleeping. We buried her in the family plot, next to my dad."

Emma embraced him again.

This time, when she held him, he let himself hold her back. He felt her slender body shake with empathetic sobs. It helped, having her share his pain and understand all he and his boys had been through. Finally, she extricated herself from the circle of his arms.

"I'm sorry I wasn't here at the time," she whispered emotionally. "But what can I do to help now?"

There was only one thing Tom wanted. Release from the last bit of guilt and remaining grief, so he could finally move on and start to think about finding a new life partner and loving mother for his boys. But since that wasn't likely to come tonight, not with her nixing further lovemaking and his boys sleeping upstairs, he said, instead, "Help with their project."

She gave him a bewildered look.

He went to his desk and got the three sets of instructions he had taken from their backpacks after school.

Her delicate brow lifted. She turned away as if they hadn't just shared an embrace that had rocked his world, and brought them even closer. "'The All About My Family pre-K project,'" she read out loud.

Tom waited for her to peruse the instructions. "They've had some issues in recent years, doing Mother's Day projects at school."

Her expression softened. "I can imagine it made them sad since their mom was gone?"

"Exactly. So the pre-K teachers got together. And decided to do something that would be a lot more inclusive, and would match the All About Me project they did at the beginning of the year."

"'It requires a poster board, with information about the child's family group,'" Emma continued reading. "'Which can include biological and nonbiological family members, of as many generations as the child would like.'"

She put the paper down. "It sounds fun. Yet you're worried."

He paused. "I don't know if I should include Vicki or not."

Emma straightened. The change in her posture pushed the round curves of her breasts up and out. "Of course, you should!"

He forced his glance away from the delectable sight. "What if it upsets them or their classmates?"

"They seem to be handling it pretty well now."

Tom moved closer but resisted the urge to sit next to her again. He didn't know what it was about Emma, but she brought out the alpha male in him. "What if it dredges stuff up?" He paced back and forth.

Emma stood, too. She handed him the instructions. "Then we will deal with it. Together."

Together. He liked the sound of that. He pivoted toward her. "That means you'll help?"

She stepped forward and hugged him fiercely, like an old and trusted friend this time. "Of course, I will."

Chapter Nine

Emma was setting out a picnic breakfast in the still-empty retail showroom for Tom and the triplets, the following morning, when her phone rang. It was Mimi Alexander, Barbara Roswald's administrative assistant. "I just want to confirm the appointment at 1:00 p.m., a week from Friday, and give you a list of the things my boss is going to want to see upon arrival…"

Grabbing a pen and paper, Emma began taking notes. She had just finished when Tom and The Alphabet Gang walked up. They grinned at her from the other side of the plate-glass windows.

She waved them in. The boys moved excitedly toward the blanket she had spread out on the floor, picnic-style, and looked at the spread. "Cinnamon rolls!" Austin said and grinned.

They were the kind you bought at the grocery store that came in a tube and then baked, but the kids acted like the freshly frosted breakfast pastries were the most delicious thing they had ever seen.

"And yogurt with fruit and stuff!" Bowie observed. She had assembled the parfaits herself.

"Can we eat it?" Crockett asked.

"Of course." Emma gestured for everyone to sit cross-legged on the floor. Paper plates and napkins were passed around, along with the silverware, yogurt cups and individual containers of milk.

She handed Tom a to-go cup of black coffee, with a lid. Her own appetite suddenly gone, she tried not to look at the pages of handwritten notes under her phone.

"Everything okay?" Tom asked.

Emma nodded. "Business." She smiled at the boys when they mugged happily at her.

"Not good?" he guessed quietly.

"Overwhelming," she murmured back.

His gaze drifted over her, exuding kindness. "Want to discuss it later?"

Did she? She knew she needed a sounding board. He had always had excellent business acumen, even when they'd been undergrads together. Since, he had taken his family's struggling ranch, expanded into Wagyu cattle and now real estate. "If you wouldn't mind…"

In the meantime, she needed to focus on the boys and the short time they had together before they went off to school for the day.

All too soon, it was time for them to go. Tom and

Get ready to relax and indulge with your **FREE BOOKS** and more!

Claim up to FOUR NEW BOOKS & TWO MYSTERY GIFTS – absolutely FREE!

Dear Reader,

We both know life can be difficult at times. That's why it's important to treat yourself so you can relax and recharge once in a while.

And I'd like to help you do this by sending you this amazing offer of up to FOUR brand new full length FREE BOOKS that WE pay for.

This is everything I have ready to send to you right now:

Try **Harlequin® Special Edition** books featuring comfort and strength in the support of loved ones and enjoying the journey no matter what life throws your way.

Try **Harlequin® Heartwarming™ Larger-Print** books featuring uplifting stories where the bonds of friendship, family and community unite.

Or **TRY BOTH!**

All we ask in return is that you answer 4 simple questions on the attached Treat Yourself survey. You'll get **Two Free Books** and **Two Mystery Gifts** from each series you try, *altogether worth over $20*! Who could pass up a deal like that?

Sincerely,

Pam Powers

Harlequin Reader Service

Treat Yourself to Free Books and Free Gifts.

Answer 4 fun questions and get rewarded.

We love to connect with our readers! Please tell us a little about you...

	YES	NO
1. I LOVE reading a good book.	◯	◯
2. I indulge and "treat" myself often.	◯	◯
3. I love getting FREE things.	◯	◯
4. Reading is one of my favorite activities.	◯	◯

TREAT YOURSELF • Pick your 2 Free Books...

Yes! Please send me my Free Books from each series I select and Free Mystery Gifts. I understand that I am under no obligation to buy anything, as explained on the back of this card.

Which do you prefer?

❑ **Harlequin® Special Edition** 235/335 HDL GRCC
❑ **Harlequin® Heartwarming™ Larger-Print** 161/361 HDL GRCC
❑ **Try Both** 235/335 & 161/361 HDL GRCN

FIRST NAME   LAST NAME

ADDRESS

APT.#   CITY

STATE/PROV.   ZIP/POSTAL CODE

EMAIL ❑ Please check this box if you would like to receive newsletters and promotional emails from Harlequin Enterprises ULC and its affiliates. You can unsubscribe anytime.

the boys disposed of all the trash, and then Emma handed out wet wipes to get the stickiness off their hands and faces.

"Thank you, Princess Lady Emma!" Crockett hugged her first. Austin and Bowie followed.

"Goodbye, Buttercup!" They knelt to give her dog a gentle embrace, too.

"Thanks for this," Tom said, as he shepherded them out the door. "It made the routine this morning a whole lot easier."

It had made her morning, too. Or at least it totally would have, had she not had that phone call.

Emma walked them as far as the door. "Glad to hear that," she replied.

She gathered up the blanket, her notes and what was left of her coffee, and headed up to her apartment. Thirty minutes later, the intercom buzzed. Not expecting any visitors, she was surprised to discover it was Tom. He must have raced right back after dropping off the kids. Feeling both relieved and excited to have him there with her again she said, "Come on up. I'm in my apartment."

She opened the door to let him in. How was it that he always knew when she needed him?

Finding refuge in their repartee, she propped one hand on her hip and intimated dryly, "You know when I said I would like to talk about it, I didn't mean right this very minute."

He flashed a reassuring grin, sauntering past her. As always, he smelled like soap and man and woodsy cologne. "No time like the present. So, what's the problem?" he said, shutting the door behind them.

She handed over the pages. "Read it and weep. I almost did."

He scanned the notes. "The buyer wants to see financial statements for the last three years, as well as a breakdown on how much it costs to produce each style of shoe or boot, how many were sold, what the cash flow was, monthly, during this time. And how much debt, if any, that you have on the books right now."

Emma twisted her hands in front of her, aware after years of waiting for what might finally be her big break, things were moving awfully quickly. She drew a calming breath, explaining why the demand had caught her off guard. "I thought—well, *hoped*— that in the initial meeting all Barbara Roswald was going to want to do was see my work space, look at my most popular design in all its iterations and learn about the process of making my wedding boot."

Tom nodded. "I'm sure she will want to do all that as well," he said matter-of-factly. "If she is serious about doing business with you, and I don't think she would want to come all the way from Chicago to see you, unless she were."

He took her by the hand and led her over to the sofa. Then, sitting down beside her, he stretched his long legs over the coffee table and folded his hands behind his head. "I am guessing from the look on your face that your records are not in great shape."

Emma sagged against the cushions. Leave it to Tom to hit the nail on the head. "They barely exist. I mean,

I filed papers with the Texas secretary of state when I started The Boot Lab and I've filed tax returns every year since, as required."

"But...?" Straightening, he searched her eyes.

Emma compressed her lips dejectedly. "I know my sales are not going to be what they want to see." The heat of humiliation filled her face. She hated the fact that after all the sacrifices she had made, when it came to her personal life, she was still so much less successful professionally than he was. Especially given the fact they had started out at the same time at the same place when they had graduated from Texas Tech with business degrees.

Now, here he was with everything she wanted. Including a family of his own.

While she was still struggling, alone.

Well, not *quite* alone. She had Buttercup—who was curled up on her cushion, napping now.

Doing her best to hide her discomfort, she waved an airy hand, continuing, "Yes, I've sold nearly five hundred lace-up wedding boots, all of which were hand-sewn by me, but a lot of my other designs have only sold a few pairs, if that."

He draped his arm along the back of the sofa, behind her. "Any reason why?"

She turned slightly toward him. His intense interest made it easy to confide. "Well, I haven't marketed them. Not to the degree of my wedding boot."

He pivoted in his seat, his knee nudging hers. She soaked in the warmth exuding from his tall, strong body. "But, if I recall correctly, it was the wedding boot that Barbara Roswald wanted to see. So, maybe you should just focus on that."

"That was my initial plan, but then her assistant Mimi Alexander called and gave me this list."

His gaze narrowed. He silently calculated. "Okay, so you go for broke and show her everything you've got. Plus, figures on everything."

Emma moaned, embarrassed to have to admit yet another shortcoming to the man who seemed to excel at everything. Except maybe cooking for his sons. She threw up a hand in frustration. "Tom, accounting never was my strong suit…"

He chuckled and flashed her a sexy grin. And this time he did pull her into the curve of his body. "Then you're lucky it has always been mine." He kissed the top of her head, squeezed her shoulder comfortingly, then drew back to look into her eyes. "I love numbers. And I *really like* making fancy charts and graphs on the computer. Not to mention, putting together perspectives for potential investors."

She could see that. Still, it was a lot to ask. She searched the inscrutable expression on his face. "You would help me with all that?"

He nodded, serious now. "Maybe that way I can repay you for all your help with the boys and make up for the unconscionable way I treated you way back when."

Emma straightened abruptly. "You were never rude to me."

"I did something a whole lot worse." Regret etched his handsome features. "I didn't support your dreams."

A brief silence fell. Given the chance to express her own remorse, Emma admitted sorrowfully, "It was a two-way street, Tom. I didn't support your responsibilities here at home, to your family's ranch, your mom…"

His eyes turned a dark golden brown. "So maybe we both made a mistake."

She nodded, glad they had finally come to a place where they could acknowledge that. "And maybe now we can move on," she murmured.

"Good with me," Tom said, in a low, gravelly voice.

The next thing she knew his hands were around her waist, and he was shifting her over onto his lap. His head slanted over hers.

Emma hadn't expected him to kiss her.

But once his lips locked tenderly on hers, she wasn't about to command him to stop, either. She needed him to do this. Needed to know once and for all if there was still something special between them. And if she was wrong, and this was just pure physical attraction, then maybe she could make hot, reckless love with him one final time and get him out of her system.

The problem was, she thought, as he kissed her over and over again, this felt so good. *He* felt so good. Especially when he shifted again, and she found herself straddling him. He swept his hands down her sides, cupping her hips. Lower still, she felt the hard, hot pressure of his desire.

He gazed at her with turbulent eyes that made her hungry for more. "Tell me this is okay…"

"More than okay…" She pressed even closer, molding her body to his. Wrapping her arms around his wide, muscular shoulders, kissing him like this, made her feel so sexy, vibrant and alive.

Like she could literally conquer the world...

Their tongues tangled and their lips melded. He kissed her as if they had never broken up, never been apart. As if he meant to have her and make her his. She loved the way he seemed to savor everything about their make-out session, even as he encouraged her to let her guard down in a way she hadn't in, well, ages.

Yearning washed over her. Wanting to feel connected to him, body and soul, she unbuttoned his shirt, slid her hands over his warm, satiny smooth chest.

"Bed?" he rasped, undoing her blouse, too.

She shook her head. Rising only long enough to whisk off her moccasins, jeans and panties. "Here."

He grinned as she reached for his belt and lifted up so, together, they could ease off his jeans. Clad only in their open shirts, she positioned herself over him once again.

The pulsing heat of his lower body ignited them both. He moved his hand down her spine until her breasts nestled against his chest. Their lips locked again, tongues entwined, and just that swiftly they were on the path to fulfillment once again. Need poured out of her, matching his own, and when his hand swept between them, finding the softness, she caught her breath. Arched. Still stroking, he gave her a long thorough kiss designed to entice her to further lower the barriers around her heart.

Even as he switched places with her, kneeling between her knees, tasting and exploring every pleasure point. Making her wild with yearning, in a way she never could have imagined.

When the shudders came, her cry of ecstasy had him grinning with masculine satisfaction. Then it was her turn to pleasure him.

Until at last there was no more waiting. He found a condom. Together, they rolled it on. And then she was straddling him, her mouth molding to the plundering pressure of his.

She was wet and open.

He was hot and hard.

And oh, how well they fit. As if he were made for her, and she for him. They gave to each other. He went deeper, slower, stronger. And then there was nothing but the ascent into sweet, hot, melting bliss.

Afterward, Emma let her head drop to his shoulder and clung to him. She felt so at home, so safe, so… loved…whenever they were together like this.

But she knew it couldn't last.

Still holding her close, he stroked a hand through her hair. "Thoughts?" He kissed the top of her head.

Regret shimmered through her. That she had let herself hope for the impossible. And maybe him, too. Reluctantly, she lifted her head and forced herself to speak what was on her mind. "As good as this was…" And it had been *spectacularly* good! "I don't think we can go back to where we were, before the breakup." His eyes darkened, and though it hurt to admit it, she made herself say the words. "Or forward, either." She drew a breath and continued holding his searching gaze. "Given the fact I'm likely leaving here, six months from now."

For a moment he didn't react at all. Finally, he shrugged. "So maybe we don't do either."

She sent a questioning look his way.

He lifted her hand to his lips and kissed the back of it. "Maybe we just live in the present, get you ready for this meeting with RTW Bridal, and don't worry about anything else."

Emma gave Tom all the financial documentation she had on her business, promising to email him the rest, and he went back to the ranch to work on sorting through it while she stayed in town and continued unpacking moving boxes.

She was beginning to wonder if and when she would ever get done when three of the ladies from Laramie Gardens arrived on Emma's doorstep, ready to be of service. "We're here to help you in whatever way you need, to get your place of business set up!" Miss Mim said, looking like the guardian angel she was.

"Just tell us what to do and where to start," Miss Isabelle beamed.

"And we will give it our all," Miss Patricia promised.

Grateful for the neighborly assistance—it was one of the perks of living in Laramie County again!— Emma showed them where the boxes of shoe molds were. "They're all numbered according to size, and I need the smallest on the top shelf, the largest, the bottom."

While they got started on that, she unpacked the bolts of leather, satin, brocade, canvas and patent leather, arranging them in a rainbow of colors.

Her tools came next.

Then the premade heels and soles she had purchased from a manufacturer in South Texas.

Finished, for the moment, all four women stepped back to admire their handiwork. "Now we're talking!" Miss Patricia exclaimed. "This looks fabulous!"

Emma knew she owed them for their assistance. It would have taken her two solid days to do what they had managed in just a few hours.

"Except...where are all your beautiful shoes?" Miss Mim asked.

"Upstairs in my apartment."

"Could we see them?" Miss Isabelle murmured.

Emma shrugged. "Sure. If you don't mind the moving mess."

After they assured her it wouldn't be a problem, Emma led the way up the back stairs, into her apartment. But she realized her guests might have spoken too soon, as they looked around at the slow-dripping kitchen faucet and dingy walls and trim. "I must say I'm surprised." Miss Isabelle harrumphed. "I thought Tom Reid would be a much better landlord."

Miss Mim agreed. "You should have insisted he paint before you took possession."

Emma waved off their concern, explaining, "He offered. I'm the one who put him off."

Miss Patricia blinked. "Why on earth would you do that, dear?"

Gesturing for the three ladies to take a seat at the dining table, Emma plugged in her electric tea kettle. "I needed to take possession right away. I figured it could be done later." *After my six months were up.*

"Well, I think you should talk to Tom and get him to do it ASAP," Miss Mim said.

The other two nodded in agreement. "Honestly, dear, this is a little depressing," Miss Patricia noted.

A tight knot of stress balled into a fist in Emma's middle. Hoping to get the women on to another topic, she began opening up the travel trunks that held her shoes and boots. "True, but there is only so much of me to go around, and right now, I am focused on opening up my studio and retail space as soon as possible."

Miss Isabelle frowned. "What difference would a few days to a week make?"

A ton, if she were not as prepared as she should be for her appointment with Barbara Roswald.

Miss Mim, who had mentored her and every other child who came through the Laramie County Public Library doors for years, immediately took notice of the stress building within Emma.

And suddenly it was all too much.

She found herself confiding in the three women everything that was at stake.

"But your designs are so gorgeous," Miss Isabelle soothed.

Miss Patricia bobbed her head in agreement. "And the bridal boots that your sister Faith wore to her wedding to Lieutenant Zach Callahan were a true showstopper!"

Emma smiled, recalling what a truly romantic evening that had been. Then she sobered. "But the world is full of pretty shoes." Hers were only a few of them.

"You think you need something to set you apart to get a deal from this company?" Miss Mim asked.

Emma handed out cups of tea and opened up a tin of sugar cookies from the Sugar Love Bakery. She passed those out too as she answered, "Something that would be overwhelming in the sense that it showcases my talent, yes."

Miss Isabelle stirred sugar into her tea. "What about a portfolio?"

"Of my shoes?" Emma got out the creamer and lemon, too. She set those on the table. "That's a great idea, but there's no time…"

"That's the beauty of it, dear. You wouldn't have to do a thing. The residents of Laramie Gardens would do it for you." Miss Mim started making calls and barking out orders like an army drill sergeant.

Before Emma knew it, the activity bus from Laramie Gardens was pulling up in front of her store. Half a dozen of the men—all of whom had recently taken up photography—stepped out. The next few hours were a flurry of activity, but by the end of the day, all of her shoes had been beautifully photographed, and the film transported to the local print shop for developing. Everyone wished her well, waved goodbye and the bus left.

Exhausted from watching all the activity, Buttercup came over to be petted. And that was when the FaceTime request from Tom came in.

Chapter Ten

"You know when you play the game Mother May I, it's one step forward, two steps back, two steps forward, one step back," he said.

Emma could hear the sounds of a huge meltdown in the background and watched as Tom stepped farther into the foyer, where it was a little bit quieter.

Emma studied his harried expression, the way his hair was standing on end, as if he had been running his hands through it. Her heart went out to him. Things had been going so well, last night and this morning! She regarded him sympathetically. "I'm guessing you are going backward right about now?"

He exhaled and made a face that indicated just how overwhelmed he felt. "Yeah."

"What happened?" she asked gently.

He rubbed the back of his neck. "They did not like the fact that we couldn't stop by to see you after school, and weren't going to see you this evening, either."

Emma paused. She thought this had all been worked out, too. "But they know they are coming here for breakfast before school tomorrow morning?"

Tom grimaced. He stopped massaging the muscles in his neck. His hand fell to his side. "It didn't mollify them in the least. And here's the thing," he admitted gruffly, "my mom is going to call to chat with them in another half an hour."

Emma studied the tumult in his eyes. "And if Marjorie sees or hears their distress, she really will be on the next flight home."

"Right," he said, as the yelling in the distance increased exponentially.

Emma paused, aware there really was no decision to be made. "Tell you what. Give me five minutes to pack up my laptop and the rest of the financial papers I found after you left this morning, and Buttercup and I will drive right out to the ranch."

His broad shoulders relaxed. He looked at her gratefully. "Thank you. So much!"

Emma chuckled. "No problem. And don't worry… you are going to pay me back once we get those little rascals fed, and in bed for the night."

He squinched his eyes. "Uh…about dinner…"

She waved off his concern. "Not to worry. I'll enlist them to help me with that, too."

Emma said goodbye then hurried out the door. Still, it took a good thirty minutes before she was turning into the drive of the Rocking R ranch. To her surprise, the boys were sitting on the porch, looking calm and happy as could be. Tom was holding the tablet.

"Here she is! Our Princess Lady Emma!" Crockett crowed happily.

Tom turned the tablet toward her and Buttercup. His mother appeared on-screen.

Emma waved. "Hey, Marjorie."

"Hello, dear. Thank you for helping out, as always."

They chatted for a few minutes. Then because it was well after midnight in Italy, Marjorie excused herself.

"Can Buttercup play in the backyard with us?" Austin asked the moment the call ended.

Emma smiled at the boys, letting them know she appreciated their offer of help. "Actually, guys, she's been cooped up in the apartment and at the design studio all day. So that would be really good for her."

"I'll get her some water," Bowie volunteered.

Emma unsnapped the leash, and she and Tom watched from beneath the covered back patio while the kids and dog raced to the swing set.

He still looked stressed.

"Seems like you were able to calm them down after all," she murmured encouragingly, knowing what it felt like when your life suddenly seemed to be reeling out of control.

He rubbed his jaw with the flat of his hand. Drawing her attention to the evening beard rimming his jaw. Damn, he was handsome, even at times like this!

Ruefully, he admitted, "Only because I told them you were coming to see us this evening after all."

She curved a hand around his biceps. That was all it took to remind her of the passionate way they had made love that very morning. "Did they give you any explanation other than that they didn't get their way?"

"No."

"But it seems like it is more than that," she observed with a note of concern. "Because I'm guessing they don't usually act out like this."

He sent her a relieved glance, seeming grateful she was there with him. "Right. I mean, they get into mischief, of course, and sometimes don't play as well with each other as I would like to see, but… The kicking, the screaming, the pounding the floor…is brand-new." And obviously not something he wanted to see continue.

Emma edged closer. "Did you ask them about it?"

"Yes." His voice took on a troubled edge. "They won't even look me in the eye."

Which meant it *was* something. Aware they had three little chaperones within eyesight, she resisted the urge to embrace their dad. Instead, she turned so her back was to the boys. "Want me to try and talk to them on my own?"

His gaze traced her upturned features. "You think you can get somewhere with them?"

The sense of intimacy between them deepened even more. "We won't know until I try," Emma said lightly, accepting the fact that for now, anyway, they were a team. And a successful one at that. "In the meantime…" She stepped inside the house and went to get the work carryall she had brought in with her. Returning, she took out a folder, leaving her laptop in the bag for now. Their fingers brushed as she handed over the papers. "This is the rest of what I could find in terms of financial records, and orders to date. So if you want to start looking through that…and see what else I'm going to need…" The brief contact caused a flurry of tingles through her entire body. "I'll go deal with the little cowpokes."

"Thanks, Emma." He brought her close for a brief, grateful hug.

"No problem. And like I said earlier on the phone—" she winked "—you're going to more than pay me back for my help. Each to our strengths, right?"

He chuckled, the light coming back into his amber eyes. "Right."

Emma went out the back door. Buttercup saw her coming, but decided to stay where she was with the three lively boys.

"Are you going to cook dinner for us?" Bowie asked, from atop the climbing fort when she strolled up to join them.

She sat down on the seat of the glider-swing for two. Austin swung back and forth on a bench swing while Crockett climbed up the stairs of the slide and Buttercup sat at attention, watching contentedly from below.

"In a little bit." Emma ran the toe of her sneakers through the playground mulch. "I wanted to talk to you guys first."

All three turned suddenly wary.

Her fingers gripping the metal chain of the glider swing, she pushed on. "Why are you giving your daddy such a hard time? You know he is trying his best."

The boys paused. "Well, sometimes you have to try harder. Go the extra mile," Crockett said finally.

That sounded like grown-up talk. "Did someone tell you that?"

All three averted their gazes.

"Not exactly," Bowie finally said.

"We're not supposed to talk about what other people say in their conversations." Crockett pushed off and slid down the slide to the ground.

"'Cause it's not polite to eavesdrop," Austin said.

Bowie shook his head in consternation. "Even if we're worried that daddy is going to mess it up *again*. The way he did the last time."

Okay. Now they were finally getting somewhere! "You mean last weekend?" she asked. "When your grandma first left on her trip?"

Crockett made a face. "No, silly. When he was going to marry you, and then he chased you away and you didn't come back to Texas for a very long time."

Oh my... Emma thought, stunned they had somehow learned about this.

"Yeah, and when you did come back, you didn't give him the time of day," Bowie added emotionally.

"Which is okay, Gramma said, because you had both moved on," Austin concluded.

"Austin!" Bowie chided his brother. "We're not *sup-*

posed to talk about what Gramma says to her friends when she is on the phone."

Emma held up a staying hand. "I think it's okay this one time," she said gently.

Buttercup nosed closer, then sat so Emma could pet her.

"So your grandma was talking to her friends…" She struggled to get a fuller picture. "And this was when…?"

"When she was packing to go on her trip," Crockett admitted importantly. "She said, she hoped that Daddy didn't blow it, and chase you away again, because you were going to help him with us. And if things went the way she hoped, he would make up for past mistakes and marry you this time…"

Oh boy.

Bowie spread his hands wide, his concern evident. "And then you didn't come to dinner tonight…"

"And Daddy said we couldn't stop by your new space, either…" Austin added.

Bowie pouted. "And you didn't sleep here last night…"

They really had put it all together—at least in their own fast-working minds. "We explained I had work to do in town this morning. And then, this afternoon, I had a lot of people at the new retail space, helping me. So your dad and I thought it would be better to wait until tomorrow morning to see each other."

The triplets took a moment to absorb that. Clearly, they hadn't bought Tom's rationale. Bowie squinted. "So you're *not* mad at daddy?"

Emma gave them her most reassuring smile. "No. Not at all," she said gently.

Austin looked like he might burst into tears at any second. "And you're not going to leave Texas again?"

This was harder to answer. "No…" Emma said, knowing it was what the boys needed to hear in this moment to feel safe and secure. "I'm not," she said quietly. *Not right now anyway.*

And if that time came, six months down the road, well then, she and Tom would have to find a way to explain it to the boys in the way they would understand.

In the meantime, though, she began to see the pitfalls of having Tom's kids depend on her, even for a couple of weeks. She had figured they would not need her once Marjorie returned from Italy. Now, she wasn't certain that would be entirely true. She frowned, wondering what she and Tom should do now.

The kids misinterpreted her unhappiness with herself. "Are you mad at us for having a meltdown?" Austin asked, his lower lip trembling.

Emma shook her head and gathered him close. Seconds later, his brothers were right there, joining in the group hug. "No," she promised, embracing them one by one. "I understand there has been a lot of change in just a few days. And you all are doing the best you can."

The boys stayed contentedly close. Big smiles crossed their faces.

"And that's all anyone can ever do," she concluded, with a surge of maternal tenderness. She loved the way they felt, snuggled in her arms. Loved the sense of family they brought to her once-lonely life.

Reluctantly, she let them go. "Now what do you say we all go inside and see about rustling up some dinner?"

The triplets perked up. "Breakfast for dinner?" Bowie asked.

Emma gathered them close again as they proceeded toward the house. "Sounds good to me!"

"So they know we were engaged?" Tom asked, several hours later when the triplets were finally in bed and asleep for the night.

Emma bypassed the dining room table, where he had spread out all her financial papers, and went into the kitchen to make a much-needed vanilla latte with a double shot of espresso.

"Yes, that's right." Wishing she weren't so darned comfortable in this house, where she'd spent so much time when she and Tom were dating, she turned her gaze from his handsome profile as he approached her. Like usual, he settled for a cup of plain black coffee. "The triplets gathered from what they overheard that Marjorie wishes we could pick up where we left off."

He put his hands on her shoulders. "I'm sorry. I had no idea this was what they were worked up about, or I wouldn't have let you talk to them."

"It's good you did. I don't think they would have told you what the real problem was." Emma added the steamed milk to her drink. "Not without hurting your feelings, which they don't want to do."

He looked her square in the eye. "So what are we going to do?"

She stirred in vanilla sugar. "Besides keep explaining that you and I are just good friends? I don't know, other than just take it one day at a time until your mother gets back…"

Which the way she was feeling could not be a moment too soon. "In the meantime—" she pushed aside the urge to kiss him again "—what did you gather from looking at the information I gave you to peruse?"

He lounged against the kitchen counter, mug in hand. "Eighty percent of your company's profit comes from the wedding boot, but only forty percent of the materials cost goes toward making it. The other sixty percent of the material costs, produce the shoes that only provide twenty percent of the overall sales."

"Wow," she said, heading back to the dining room, and the stacks of paperwork there. "I knew the financials were lopsided, but I had no idea it was that bad."

He sat opposite her at the dining room table. As they settled, their knees brushed. Tingling, she scooted her chair back. "What do you think I should do? Given that I want to appear as successful as possible to garner their interest. While still letting them know that I'm capable of designing and producing more than just boots."

"I would suggest separating out the wedding boot, as the primary source of revenue. Maybe categorize everything else as products that are still being developed. And so, aren't expected to be profitable just yet."

She reached across the table to take his hand. "That's a great idea. Thank you for helping."

He grinned amicably. "Thank *you* for helping." His eyes lit up with gratitude...but the way his gaze roved over her face conveyed much more. "Now let's get to work!"

Tom saw Emma begin to fade around midnight. "You sure you don't want to call it quits for today?" he said.

Even Buttercup was sound asleep, beneath the table, stretched out and snoring lightly.

She cast an affectionate glance at her new pet, as deeply maternal toward the labradoodle as she was to his sons, before turning back to him. "We don't have that much more to do, compiling all the sales figures on the various shoes. I'd rather get it done tonight."

He reached across the table and melded his fingers with hers. "You're exhausted."

She squeezed his fingers in return, then extricated her hand and lifted both arms above her head, stretching out the muscles in her upper back and shoulders. "I just need another cup of coffee. And I'll be fine."

He turned his glance from the soft swell of her breasts, and got up. Determined to be the gentleman he had been raised to be. "At least let me make it for you," he said.

Weariness etched her smile. "If you insist..."

"I do."

She slid back her chair. "I'm going to walk around and try to stretch out the rest of my muscles."

Happy she was taking a break, he went into the kitchen. She wasn't in the dining room when he returned. Neither was Buttercup. Thinking maybe she had taken her dog out—via the front door this time—he walked into the foyer and spotted them both. Emma was slumped over on one end of the living room sofa, sound asleep. Buttercup was curled up in front of her, also snoozing. He set down their coffees. His gaze drifted over her pink cheeks and tousled mane of chestnut hair. "Emma?" he said softly.

Stirring only slightly, she inhaled and stretched out on the sofa. He adjusted the pillows beneath her head. Then gently removed her shoes. Covered her with a blanket. And felt his own emotions stir.

Damn, she was beautiful. Strong and yet fragile, too. So very womanly. And miracle of miracles, she was back in his life again. Maybe to stay...?

Turning out the light, he headed for bed himself, his heart full.

Chapter Eleven

"I told you making a wish would work!" Crockett said when he dashed down the stairs and saw Emma and Buttercup were still there.

Embarrassed to find she had spent yet another night on Tom's sofa, unplanned this time, she struggled to sit up. Her entire body was sluggish with fatigue, but the delighted expressions on the boys' faces warmed her through and through.

Buttercup stretched and rose, her tail wagging. The boys reciprocated with rousing good mornings to her, too.

Looking relaxed and at ease, Tom came into the room. "What wish?" he asked, having caught the tail end of his son's exuberant conversation.

"That Princess Lady Emma would be here for breakfast!" Crockett said.

There it was again. Her dreaded childhood nickname. Yet, just as when they had used it the very first time, it no longer rankled. In fact, it was absolutely endearing, coming from Tom's little boys.

"We like it when she has a sleepover with us," Bowie said with enthusiasm.

"So we *wished* that she would and she did," Austin concluded happily, sitting next to Emma for a cuddle. He beamed up at her.

It was impossible not to smile down at him, too. Even though she knew this was a path they should not be on. "What time is it?" she asked, not quite sure where she had left her phone.

Tom glanced at his watch. "Seven forty-five."

She looked down at her sleep-wrinkled clothing and tousled hair. "Oh no."

His dark brow lifted. "What?"

Emma shot to her feet, and headed for the dining room and the mess of papers still there. "I'm supposed to meet Travis at the shop at eight! He's going to deliver the display stands and put up the shelves."

He sent her a sympathetic glance. "You'll never make it."

Spying her phone on top of a stack of papers, she reached for it. "I'll just text him that I'm running late. Move it to nine…"

Tom kicked into gear too. "Listen fellas, how about we give Emma a moment to pull herself together?" He turned back to her. "I'll take Buttercup out, give her water and some of the extra food you left here, while the boys grab some breakfast." He directed his sons toward the kitchen. "The cereal and milk is already on the kitchen table. You all know what to do."

"Okay, Daddy." They rushed off, and Tom and Emma went their separate ways as well.

Glad she always carried a toothbrush and tube of paste, plus hairbrush and face soap in her carryall, Emma slipped into the bathroom. There was nothing she could do about her sleep-wrinkled clothing since she did not have a change of clothes with her. But five minutes later, she looked and felt a lot better.

She opened the door. All three boys were waiting impatiently for her. "We got a surprise," Bowie announced.

"And you're going to love it," Austin predicted.

Crockett took her by the hand. "Come on. We will show you."

They led her into the kitchen. "Daddy said you're in too much of a hurry to eat breakfast with us." Crockett frowned.

"But Gramma says breakfast is the most important meal of the day," Bowie put in.

"So, we fixed it for you, so you can eat, and then run."

Indeed they had. A cereal bowl had been one-third filled with the shredded wheat she had chosen the night they had cereal for dinner, half a pint of blueberries and enough milk to fill it nearly to the brim. A glass of orange juice had been poured, also to the rim, some of it sloshing over the sides.

"Wow," Emma said, simultaneously stunned and touched. "This looks delicious, guys."

"We knew you would like it!" Austin beamed.

Seeing no way out of it, she helped the boys fill their own bowls with whatever cereal and fruit combo they wanted, then sat down and began to eat. Tom came in, Buttercup trotting happily at his side.

"We cooked for Emma again!" Bowie reported.

Tom caught her eye, a myriad of complex emotions in his expression. Paternal pride. Surprise. And worry…that everyone might be getting a little too attached to having her at the Rocking R. "I see." With a playful wink, he asked, "Where's mine?"

Bowie waved off the hint. "We only had time to cook for Princess Lady Emma."

The corners of their dad's lips twitched slightly as he gazed over at her bowl. "My loss." He gave Emma another look, this one the intimate kind one parent gave another. And not for the first time, she knew what it would be like to be part of this crazy, rambunctious, wonderful family.

To Emma's consternation, even though she made it back to town with fifteen minutes to spare, her brother Travis was already there, parked next to the service entrance at the rear of The Boot Lab.

Damn. She could tell by his ornery grin he was not going to let this go.

"Emma! Really?" he teased, getting out of his truck. He mugged at her comically. "The walk of shame?"

She held up a silencing palm. "It's not what you think."

"Kind of looks like you're still wearing what you were wearing yesterday."

She tried and failed to completely contain a guilty flush. "Everyone sleeps in their clothes from time to time, bro."

"Mmm-hmm. At the Rocking R again?"

"On their sofa. And yes. *Again*. It's not what you think." Last night, anyway.

She unlocked the door and Travis carried his tools inside.

"So, you're not getting back together with him?" he asked.

Was she?

She knew what she wanted, a lot more moments like the ones she had with Tom and the boys this morning. She also knew that realistically that might not happen. That by the time the holidays rolled around this year she could be living and working somewhere else.

Emma focused on switching on the overhead lights. "He needs help with his kids, in Marjorie's absence. I promised his mom I would assist. And in return, Tom is helping me put together a sophisticated financial assessment for my business. So, it's a win-win."

Her brother's brow furrowed. For a moment, he looked as protective of her as he had been when he had first come to live with Carol and Robert, and she had been, at age three, a persistent little shadow to her emotionally guarded thirteen-year-old brother. He motioned for her to come with him to his truck, so she could help him carry in the brackets while he hefted the actual shelving. "Just be careful," he said, suddenly serious. "I don't want you having your heart broken again."

Suddenly, she had the feeling they were no longer talking about her situation. Emma took as much as she could handle, then headed for the service door, which they had left propped open. "Tom's not Alicia, Travis."

He followed her back into the retail space, and gently set down the heavy load he carried. "The situations look similar to me."

Emma stacked the brackets next to that, and went back outside with him. "Tom and I aren't fixing up a property together, the way you and Alicia did." Although it hadn't started out that way. Travis had merely been a contractor for Alicia.

They picked up a second load, and headed back into the building. Travis continued to worry. "One thing can lead to another when there is a basic attraction and you're in close proximity of each other."

Is that all her brother thought she and Tom had been?

Telling herself that even now, with all the parameters they had put in place, she and Tom had more than that, Emma countered, "Tom and I never moved in together, the way you and Alicia did." They had always maintained their own spaces, even when it meant rooming with other people. "And we're not going to, either."

Travis studied her in concern, his love for her apparent. "Just make sure that you don't. Because I wouldn't want to see you do what I did and mistake a mutual temporary need for something much deeper. Only to get dumped in the end when the 'project' that brings you together is over."

The rest of Thursday afternoon, Emma thought about what her brother had said. And she was still thinking about it when Travis called it quits and headed out, promising to be back the next day to finish putting together the tiered wooden stands.

Maybe he was right. Perhaps they were all moving too fast, building a temporary family that would eventually dissolve once her career and Tom's life had them going different ways again.

Should they take a step back before the kids' expectations were raised even higher?

Unfortunately, she had already told the boys she and Buttercup would have dinner with them that evening. So, she arranged to meet in the town park for a picnic dinner that she happily provided. The kids played on the playground afterward while Buttercup watched the shenanigans, and she and Tom sat on a bench and talked about the financial prospectus that he was putting together for her.

Because she wasn't going out to the Rocking R that night, she had brought a couple of her nieces' and nephews' favorite stories and read them to Austin, Crockett and Bowie before they left Laramie.

The boys weren't overjoyed she wasn't going home with them. But they did love the books about trucks, dinosaurs and a lost bunny, and Tom promised them cookies and milk before bed if they were good listeners, so there wasn't too much complaining as their dad put them in his Silverado quad cab.

He paused before getting in himself. "Thanks for tonight," he said.

She smiled. "You're welcome."

"Breakfast tomorrow?"

This was all getting dangerously tempting. "Probably not a good idea, since Travis will be at my place bright and early."

Although she hadn't told Tom about the warning from her brother, he knew her well enough to sense something was up. "How's the installation going?" he asked casually thereby opening the door for anything else she chose to tell him.

"The shelves are up, but he still has to assemble all the tiered shoe display stands, which he estimates will take most of tomorrow."

"Does he need help?"

She waved off his offer of assistance and backed up, signaling it was time for him to go. She smiled, and peering into the passenger compartment gave the boys, who were watching them intently, another merry wave adieu.

They waved excitedly in return.

She turned back to Tom, doing her best to keep it casual. "Thanks, but there's nothing I can't do."

Tom wasn't sure what he had done to prompt Emma to put him in the just-good-friends zone again. Unless it was what the kids had said. All he knew for certain was that once again, her heart was tightly under wraps. And that if it were up to her, there would be no more intimate chitchat, or sinfully sexy looks. No casual touching or passionate kisses, or anything else that would lead them astray.

Fortunately for both of them, he was not interested in going backward. To the time when their closeness had eroded to nothing.

They'd made progress, rekindling their relationship and reigniting their passion.

He wanted that to continue.

Wanted to have even more time alone together.

Luckily, the stars had aligned to make that happen, too.

Late Friday afternoon, Tom was just headed into The Boot Lab, as Travis was packing up his tools.

Tom looked around admiringly. "Looks great in here." The shelves on both side walls of the showroom were as beautifully crafted as the three-tiered wooden display boxes.

Travis, usually a gregarious guy, merely grunted in reply. Tom took in the depth of Emma's brother's scowl and averted glance. He braced his hands on his hips. Confusion reigned. "Did I do something wrong?"

The other man shut the lid of his toolbox. Stood. And looked Tom right in the eye. "Hurt her again, the way you did the last time, and you'll answer to me," he said shortly.

Tom was not about to let the accusation go unanswered. He moved to block Travis's path to the door. "I have no intention of hurting Emma," he stated plainly.

Travis scoffed. "Yeah, well, you know what they say, the road to hell is paved with good intentions." He shouldered past and headed out the door.

Moments later, Emma came down the back stairs, through the workshop and into the retail space, checkbook in hand. Her delicate brows knit in surprise. "Where is Travis?" she asked.

Trying not to think about what he would *really* like to do, which was gather her close and forget the plans he'd already made for the evening, Tom said, "He left."

"Why? He knew I was going to pay him!"

Tom saw no need to sugarcoat the situation. Even if it wouldn't win him any points with the incredibly sexy, smart and beautiful woman standing in front of him. He shrugged. "Guess he didn't want to stand around making conversation with me."

Emma moved closer, tilting her chin up at him. She bit into the lush softness of her lower lip. "Why not? What exactly did my brother say to you?"

Tom didn't want to worry her. Especially since time would prove his intentions were extremely honorable. He waved her question aside. "Nothing to worry about."

Her dark green eyes took on the stubborn glint he knew so well. "If you don't tell me," she warned softly, "Travis will."

"Fine…if you must know…he warned me not to hurt you. I gather he thinks I am taking advantage of your kindness and generosity."

Emma shoved a hand through her hair, pushing it off her face. "Oh, Lord."

"Does this mean you don't agree with his assessment of the situation?" Because she had sort of been behaving as if she did.

She made a face. "Of course, I don't."

Good to hear.

"He is just upset, because our helping each other out has brought up his ex and the way Alicia used him as a means to an end when she was flipping that house over in San Angelo."

Tom had heard about that. Apparently, the breakup had been nasty. "Is Travis still carrying a torch?"

Emma led the way into the workroom, where they weren't in view of anyone passing by the big plate-glass store windows, and there were more comfortable places to sit. "I don't think so." She gestured for Tom to make himself comfortable, too. "He's just doubly wary. You know how it is when you get your heart smashed to smithereens. Sometimes you don't recover, or at least not for a while. I, of course, still hope he does." For the first time, she seemed to note he'd brought his laptop case with him and a thick sheaf of papers. And that school had been dismissed half an hour ago. "Where are the boys?"

"They had an after-school birthday party that includes a pizza dinner and a movie. They don't get picked up until seven thirty."

A smile spread across her face. "Wow. You must feel footloose and fancy-free," she teased.

"I could. If you will agree to go to dinner with me."

Emma's expression changed, becoming wary once again. "That's really sweet of you, but…" She rubbed at any imaginary spot on the table, and her lips took on a conflicted twist. "I don't know if that is a good idea."

So there *was* something wrong. He surveyed her loose tousled hair and pink cheeks. "Why not?"

Buttercup was standing on the staircase, looking yearningly up at the second floor. Noticing, Emma said, "I think she needs water. It's up there."

She led her pet upstairs.

Tom followed, his gaze tracking the subtle sway of her hips beneath her light gray leggings and long sleeved white T-shirt. He caught up with her at the top of the stairs. Catching a drift of her citrusy perfume, he joined her inside her apartment. "You didn't answer my question."

Emma spun back to face him. She folded her arms across her chest, every feminine defense in place. Defiantly, she met his eyes and countered with an aloof smile. "I think it's pretty obvious."

Buttercup went straight to her dishes and began to drink thirstily. His frustration growing, Tom edged closer. "To you, maybe."

She drew a bolstering breath that lifted and lowered the shapely lines of her breasts. "You heard what the boys wished yesterday morning when they found me sleeping on the living room sofa again."

He folded his arms in front of him, too, as they squared off. "So?" He shrugged, aware he liked her glossy chestnut hair down as much as he liked it up. "I'm not the only one who thinks having you around is the best way to start any day."

The corners of her lips curved down slightly. "They

can't get used to me being with all of you whenever they aren't in pre-K."

He caught the hint of worry in her low tone. Wishing he could kiss her again, without driving her away, he responded equably, "They won't. In fact, when I picked them up at school today, they were absolutely fine being away from you tonight."

She lifted a dissenting brow. "That's because they have something better to do."

His gaze drifted over the hollow of her throat, to the curve of her soft lips, to her eyes. "So, I'll arrange more playdates. Everyone's been very eager to help out since Mom's been in Italy."

She stared at him, clearly not sure what to make of that. "Why haven't you taken them up on it?"

Because I wanted us to be with you.

Not sure where that thought had come from, although he had to admit the sentiment was true, he gestured casually. "I didn't want to impose."

A brief silence fell between them. Still studying him, she tilted her head. The movement inundated him with another intoxicating drift of her citrusy, orange-blossom scent. "But counting on me isn't imposing?"

Busted.

"I didn't think it was," he rushed to say. "In fact, it's felt completely right having you in my life again, getting to know my kids."

"To me, too," she whispered, looking more conflicted than ever.

Were those tears about to fall? He cupped her shoulders between his palms and gazed down at her. His protective instincts surging, he searched the pretty contours of her face, and asked her softly, "Then what's the problem?"

Her lower lip trembled. "If we do find out we're a bad match after all, *again*, this time you and I won't be the only two who are hurting. Your boys are going to be really upset, with both of us."

"So, we won't give them a reason to be."

She gave him an apprehensive smile "Tom…"

Talking wasn't the answer. Action was. He caught her by the wrist and pulled her close. Placing one hand on her waist, weaving the other through her hair, he guided her against him, softness to hardness, woman to man.

She jerked in a ragged breath, and he could tell she felt the jolt of pure passion, too. "Tom…"

He captured her lips, kissing her deeply, persuasively. Words weren't always the best way. Sometimes it was better to show someone how you felt.

He kissed her temple, her brow, the U of her collarbone, the need to make her his again stronger than ever. Combing his fingers through her hair, he trailed his lips across her cheek before lingering on the sensitive place behind her ear. With a soft sigh of surrender, she wreathed her arms around his shoulders and settled more intimately against him.

With the intoxicating scent of her fueling his senses, he guided her backward to the wall. His head lowered, and he fused his mouth to hers, stroking and caressing the sweet cavern with the tip of his tongue. Until she was kissing him back just as evocatively, and all he could think about, all he could feel, was her firm body pressed against him. Through the thin fabric of her T-shirt, her nipples beaded against the muscles of his chest. Arousing him until his whole body ached.

Craving more, he slid his hand beneath the hem of her shirt, easing it behind her to undo the clasp of her bra. She moaned as his palms captured her silky breasts. Lust poured through him. Along with the need to claim more than just her body.

Now that he was finally fully healed from his wife's death, deep down he wanted the connection that he and Emma shared to mean more than just a hookup. He wanted it to be a gateway to the future. *Their* future. And he was sure if she would just allow herself to open up her heart again, that she would want this, too.

Emma had known Tom would eventually put the moves on her again. Just as she knew that when he did, she would give in to temptation, throw her reservations aside and kiss him back. Not just once but again and again and again.

As he tenderly meshed his lips with hers, emotion coursed through her. She had never felt such incredible need for him as she felt right now. Or felt quite as wanted in return.

When he tucked an arm beneath her knees and lifted her against his broad chest, cradling her close, she laughed shakily.

Clinging to him as he carried her into the bedroom, breathless anticipation spiraled through her as he set her down next to her bed.

"I should have known I could not resist you," she

whispered when he caught her around the waist, pulling her snug against him, one of his knees riding erotically between her thighs.

"We can't resist each other," he growled between long, lingering kisses, "and maybe that's not such a bad thing."

The next thing she knew her clothes were coming off. His followed. He dropped her onto the bed, following her down. She rolled so she was on top.

Seeming content to let her call the shots, at least initially, he nipped at her lower lip. Then slowly, languorously, ran his hands over her spine, pressing her into the hard planes of his body. In turn, she rubbed against his erection, a whimper of need escaping her. They kissed again, with soul-shattering finesse. She shuddered as he flipped her onto her side, and his mouth found her breasts, his fingertips probing the velvety warmth between her thighs.

She was wet, waiting, *wanting*. Wild in a way she could never have imagined herself being.

And, to her delight, Tom could not seem to get enough of her. He stopped long enough to grab a condom, and then he was back, easing her beneath him, lifting her hips, spreading her knees with his. Then, staring into her eyes, he penetrated her slowly, going deeper, his palms moving across her abdomen to her thighs. She arched as he plunged and withdrew and plunged again.

Wrapping her arms and legs around him, she kissed him as they moved together. Again and again. Until there was no more thinking, just acceptance and surrender and this incredible moment in time. And Emma knew as they reached release, that nothing—and no one—had ever felt so right. Or ever would.

"You know we still have time for a quick dinner out, if we hurry," Tom said when they had caught their breath.

Ignoring her first instinct, which was to stay here, wrapped in his arms, she instead eased from the bed.

Emma knew she wasn't supposed to be complicating their lives unnecessarily here. She should be sticking to the original plan. Figuring out a way for them to go back to being friends while gearing up for the biggest business opportunity of her life.

But rather than exhibiting her usual levelheadedness, she kept finding herself surrendering to temptation with this hot, sexy, ruggedly handsome man.

Sighing, she reached for the clothing she had been wearing. Scooping it off the floor, she sat on the edge of the bed to dress. Her back to him, she said, "It's one thing when we have the boys with us, and we're seen around town, grabbing a bite to eat. Quite another when it is just the two of us."

Sleepy-eyed, content, he lay back against the pillows and folded his arms behind his head. "I don't care what anyone else thinks."

She reached for her leggings, stood and shimmied into them. To her embarrassment, he was still watching, enjoying the show.

"Well, you should," Emma huffed. "People talk. Including parents of other kids."

To her frustration, he did not look the least bit worried. He grinned at her good-naturedly.

She pulled the T-shirt over her head. Frowning, continued, "For instance…someone might say something that their kid overhears and repeats at pre-K. And don't tell me it can't happen after what your boys parroted about Marjorie's private conversation with a friend yesterday. None of us need any more meltdowns of that kind."

Tom sighed, sat up and reached for his boxer briefs. "So you want to have a clandestine affair with me, is that it?"

As her eyes drifted over him, she caught a glance of his arousal, which was impossible to ignore. Tamping down the reckless warmth spiraling through her, Emma pushed aside the desire to make love again and held her ground. "I want… Hell. I don't know *what* I want!"

He nodded and made fast work of tugging on his jeans, zipping up his fly and fastening his belt. Then he closed the distance between them. "That's okay," he assured her. "We don't need to know right now. All we have to do is get by day by day until my mom gets back from Italy, and then we'll have time to figure everything out."

He reached over to straighten her pendant and tucked a strand of hair behind her ear. "And speaking of which…tomorrow is the annual Laramie Multiples Club field trip to the San Antonio Zoo."

Emma found a brush and ran it through her hair. "Is that the one where they rent luxury buses?"

"Yep." Tom straightened his hair with his fingers. "And we happen to have an extra ticket that would have gone to my mom. But since she's not here," he said, ambling closer, "you could go with us."

And feel like even more of a family than they were already starting to? Risk hurting the boys? Because there was no way they wouldn't take that adventure as a serious sign. As might others as well. Emma knelt to tie her sneakers. "I don't think so."

He sat on the edge of her bed to put on his boots. "You sure?"

She straightened the covers on her bed. "I made plans with my sisters-in-law Allison and Susannah, and sisters Faith, Jillian and Mackenzie."

He went to the other side and pulled those up, too. Together, they replaced the pillows. "Sounds like a real hen party," he drawled.

It would be. Seeing the opportunity to move the conversation to a less stressful subject, Emma teased, "Don't let them hear you saying that."

Resolutely, Tom came toward her. He stood, towering over her. All strong, indomitable male. "Seriously, we will miss you."

And I will miss you-all, too.

But not about to go there, she kept her feelings to herself, and said instead, "We'll still see each other when we work on the boys' family posters, right?"

"Right." A flash of disappointment crossed his face. He followed her out of the bedroom.

Emma signaled for Buttercup to come with them,

and escorted them both down the stairs. "When did you want to do that?"

He cocked his head. "Sunday around one o'clock okay with you, out at the ranch?"

"Sounds great."

And here they were, getting more and more involved again. With every step she took away from him, she felt herself being drawn back in. But for all their sakes, she forced herself to keep her heart under lock and key. "Didn't you come over here to show me the financial report you are working on?"

Tom grabbed his laptop case. "I did."

Relieved they had something else to focus on, Emma smiled gratefully. "Then let's get to it."

Chapter Twelve

Early Saturday morning, Emma welcomed her three sisters and two sisters-in-law to her apartment, with fresh coffee and a tray of assorted pastries. All were in work clothes and old sneakers.

"I don't get why you didn't insist that Tom have this painted before you moved in a week ago," Cade's wife, Allison, said, casting a glance at the horribly dingy walls, and the still-slow-dripping kitchen sink faucet.

If I had known I was going to catch this much grief on the subject, maybe I would have, Emma thought.

"And do you want me to take a look at that faucet, maybe put in a new washer?" Allison, a home fix-it pro on par with Martha Stewart, said.

"Anything dripping that much is really going to up your water bill," Susannah sympathized kindly.

The last thing Emma wanted was Tom underfoot unnecessarily. It was hard enough to protect her heart, and keep things casual, as it was. "It needs a whole new apparatus. The part's on order. Should be in by the end of next week, and it will be put on when it gets in." Purposefully not saying by whom, she set out the cans of paint she had picked up at the hardware store.

"And the reason I didn't wait to get the place painted was I was in a hurry to move in," she added.

"Living on the ranch with Mom and Dad got to you that much, hmm?" the ever-independent Jillian teased.

Faith bit her lip, in the way she did whenever she was trying not to divulge a secret. Realizing the director of financial services, at the area's premiere senior living center, might have heard something from the Laramie Gardens residents, Emma looked at her sister, saw the guilt in her eyes. Sighing in exasperation, she guessed, "You heard about my big meeting, didn't you?"

Faith shrugged her shoulders slightly. Admitting nothing.

Figuring word was bound to get out anyway, Emma let the matter drop and told the five women about Ready To Wear Bridal's interest in her wedding boot. "Their head buyer, Barbara Roswald, is coming to Laramie on Friday to see my studio and retail space."

"Ah, now I understand the rush to get in the space, whether it was totally ready or not," said Susannah, Gabe's wife, who was a pet portrait artist with her own in-home studio.

Emma added brushes and rollers to the stack. "The

thing is I really don't want Mom and Dad to know about the meeting."

"How come?" Mackenzie asked.

"They want me to succeed so badly…"

"You're afraid they will be disappointed if it doesn't work out the way you hope," Faith guessed gently.

"And if it does—" Emma forced herself to be as optimistic as she felt she needed to be "—then it would be a very nice surprise."

"Of course, we'll keep the meeting on the QT," Mackenzie promised.

Faith put out the drop cloths. "The portfolio the seniors helped you make might be another matter indeed. Word about that could get out."

"What portfolio?" Susannah wrinkled her nose.

"Oh, for heaven's sake," Emma said, beginning to get a little irked at having so many people in her business. She opened up the linen closet and brought out the compilation of her designs.

"Oh my word, this is gorgeous!" Mackenzie said, thumbing through them.

"Yeah, it really showcases your work," Faith added admiringly.

"Why didn't you do one before now?" Susannah asked.

"Honestly, I didn't think about investing in a lot of photos, since I usually just took the actual shoes to the trunk shows. But when Miss Mim and the others recommended it, I realized it probably would help make a positive impression to potential clients."

Allison peered at her. "You weren't insulted when they suggested it?"

Emma knew the enormously successful lifestyle blogger preferred doing her own thing, her own way. As had Emma up to now. With a sigh, she confessed, "Actually, I wish I had thought of it sooner. But I've been so focused on the actual construction and comfort of my shoes and boots, I haven't paid as much attention to marketing efforts as I should have."

"More of a presence on the fashion scene would help," Susannah agreed.

"As would some work on your current social media pages," Mackenzie said.

Emma's skills in that regard were limited. "I really can't afford to hire a web designer right now."

"You don't have to," Allison told her. "I can update your current pages in no time!"

"And I can set you up on some of the promotional sites that feature my antique rose business," Jillian said.

Susannah offered her services as well. "I built my business slowly, mostly through word of mouth, but I have several thousand contacts now. I can send out an email blast announcement, let them all know when you're going to be open for business. All you have to do is give me the details."

Emma looked at her family gratefully. "Thank you all so much!" she said.

Faith smiled. "I don't know if you need assistance with any of the financial or accounting stuff, but I could help with a lot of that."

"Actually, Tom is doing that part for me," Emma said.

For a moment it was as if they were playing a game of Statue. Everyone froze. Then looks were exchanged.

"Is that why you're painting the apartment? Instead of having him or his contractors do it? So you'll be even, in a money sense, I guess?" Faith asked.

Was it?

"I guess," Emma said.

Jillian waggled her brows suggestively. "Well, this has got to be good," she teased.

Even more heat crept into Emma's face. "It's not like that," she protested, a little too emphatically.

"Uh-huh." Mackenzie taped around the windows. "Then why are you blushing?" she demanded.

Emma knew the women in her family. They weren't going to let this go unless she gave them something. "Okay. You are all correct. Things have changed between Tom and me since he became my landlord. We have buried the hatchet and are… I guess, friends."

Susannah peered at her. "Friends or something more?"

"You're blushing again." Faith giggled.

Emma threw up her hands in exasperation. "And you're all prying!"

"Hey, I think it is great if the two of you get back together again," Jillian said gently.

"Except," Emma countered, "we're…not."

The room fell silent again. Everyone waited.

"If this thing works out with Ready To Wear Bridal, the way I hope, I will likely be leaving Laramie County again. And Tom's going to be here. In Texas. With his ranch and his business and his boys."

Strangely, none of the women around her saw that as a problem.

Were they right? Was it possible that she and Tom might be able to find a way to work things out now, unlike they had in the past? Emma didn't know. But it was certainly something to think about.

"You look pretty energetic for someone who spent all day yesterday painting an apartment," Tom noted Sunday afternoon.

She paused on the front porch of the Rocking R ranch house. Buttercup sat down, too. Wondering if Tom had missed her as much as she had missed him in the near forty-eight hours they had been apart, Emma gripped the end of the leash. She looked him over. He was dressed as nicely as if they were going on a date. In a tan button-up shirt and dark jeans and boots. He had shaved closely, too.

As for her, she had on a pretty spring dress and a pair of her fancier boots.

Curious, she propped a hand on her hip. "How do you know what I was doing yesterday afternoon?"

"Travis texted me."

Emma fought the tide of emotion rising inside her. "Oh no." Dread sifted through her. Swallowing, she forced herself to continue. "What did he say?"

Tom's gaze narrowed, his expression grave. "That I wasn't living up to my duties as a responsible landlord if you had to paint the apartment yourself."

Her breath hitched in her throat. There were times when coming from a close-knit brood was a real pain. A fact that was made worse because she was the youngest of eight. And everyone still thought they had to watch over her. Especially Travis, who had taken it upon himself to be her biggest protector, from the moment he had rejoined their family, and she had started shadowing him.

She moved close enough to feel the heat emanating from his big, powerful body. "First of all, it wasn't just me, and Travis knows that! My two sisters-in-law and three sisters were all there to help me. And it was fun. It gave us all a chance to catch up and spend a little time together."

His expression turning even more serious, he pivoted to better see her face. "Still…you have a lot going on right now, with the business…"

No denying that. Or that she had ulterior motives for not wanting Tom involved. Emma lifted her chin to meet his empathetic gaze. "It's not like it's a first, Tom. We all helped Mackenzie when she and Griff bought their fixer-upper in Fort Worth." That had been fun, too.

"Still," he said, making no bones about the fact his masculine pride had been injured. "You should have told me you wanted the place painted now, rather than later. I would have handled it for you."

"I know that," Emma admitted reluctantly. "But you were busy and I decided I better get it finished before Barbara Roswald visits the studio on Friday."

His brow lifted in surprise. "You're planning on inviting her up to the apartment?"

"I don't know," Emma confessed, raking her teeth across her lower lip. "I thought it would be better, if it were in good shape, just in case. As for Travis, you're going to have to ignore him. He's just feeling protective of me."

Tom exhaled. "I gathered."

"Tell me he didn't say anything else."

He held his poker face. Nevertheless, she knew how hard this had to be on him. He wasn't used to being accused of being ungallant.

His expression turning even more brooding, Tom confessed, "He just reiterated what he said the other day. He doesn't want to see me hurt you, even inadvertently, or take advantage."

Emma took him into her arms and said fiercely, "You're *not* going to hurt me."

"Damn right I'm not." He gathered her even closer and kissed her. "You and I have already done enough of that."

"True."

He kissed her again, even more passionately this time. She was trembling when he let her go. Had they been alone, they likely would have made love. But they weren't, so... Emma flattened a hand over the center of his chest, and slipped out of the cage of his arms. "Where are the boys?"

"Out back."

He led the way into the house. She fell in step beside him, aware how much she had missed the boys, too. Had they missed her? "How are they?"

He grinned, and said, "See for yourself."

Austin was swinging lazily back and forth. Crockett was lounging on the top floor of the play fort. Bowie was lying down, too, at the bottom of the slide. They looked like every ounce of energy had been siphoned out of them. Stunned, Emma turned back to Tom, her shoulder lightly brushing his arm in the process. "Are they going to be able to do their My Family projects?"

Tom gestured, unsure. "Here's hoping. Because they're due tomorrow."

Tom stepped off the patio and into the grass. "Hey, guys! Look who's here!"

"Princess Lady Emma!" Crockett cried.

Austin's face lit up. "Our favorite friend!"

"And Buttercup!" Bowie declared, deliriously happy.

All three came running. Buttercup dashed off, too, meeting them halfway. A total lovefest ensued.

Tom let it play out then waved them all inside. He had already set up the poster boards on the family room floor. Their names were stenciled across the top.

Below that were the words, *My Family*.

The rest was blank.

Fortunately, their dad had plenty of pictures printed out for them. The boys started with Marjorie, and Tom. Using glue sticks to affix them to the poster board in what was going to be a never-ending circle. Then they put individual pictures of the three of them on each board. Tom showed them photos of their mom, with all three of her boys.

Crockett frowned. "I don't want that one, Daddy."

"Me, neither," Bowie said.

Austin looked equally reluctant.

"Why not?" Tom asked, perplexed.

"Because she's not here anymore," Crockett said in exasperation.

"Maybe not so you can see her, but we can all still feel her love," Tom told them gently.

Emma knew he was trying to keep them from being hurt, by not having a mom in their presentation of their family. The boys were unwittingly doing the same thing, in trying to avoid the subject of their late mother altogether. "It might be uncomfortable, answering questions," she murmured quietly.

He slanted her a worried look, replying gruffly, "Doesn't mean they won't come up anyway."

True.

In this sense, the boys were going to be damned if they did, and damned if they didn't. Finally, Austin spoke up. "I want to put a picture of Princess Lady Emma on my poster."

"Me, too!" his brothers said in unison.

"And we need a photo of Buttercup!" Bowie said. They all agreed about that, too.

Oh boy, Emma thought, feeling incredibly guilty to have been chosen over Vicki. This was not what should be happening. Not at all!

"I'm not sure…" she started uncertainly, only to see the boys' faces all grow petulant.

"Our teachers said that we should tell about people

we spend time with, who we love, and love us, too," Crockett said stubbornly.

"Because that's what makes them *family*," Bowie emphasized.

"And we spend time with Emma and Buttercup and we love them!" Austin declared. He turned to Emma and continued fiercely. "And you love us, too!"

"*Don't* you?" Crockett asked.

Emma saw the concern Tom was trying to hide. She knew they had agreed that they didn't want his kids in the middle of whatever this was. But here they were. And she couldn't lie. Not with them all looking at her for confirmation, their hearts on their sleeves.

"Of course, I love you," she said, embracing them all. "And Buttercup and I would be honored to have our photo on your boards. Along with anyone else you want to include."

Except, as it turned out, they didn't want to include anyone else. Not even Vicki. It was Buttercup and Emma, Tom and Marjorie and all three boys, and that was it.

An hour later, the posters were complete and ready to take to school the next day. The boys were exhausted and wanted to watch a movie. They chose an animated version of *Cinderella*. Probably because it was one of Marjorie's favorites, Emma thought, and they missed their grandmother.

Watching the movie would help them feel close to her.

Emma made them popcorn, and Tom got out the apple juice.

Fifteen minutes in, the boys all nodded off, one by one. Emma and Tom eased off the sofa. She gathered up the empty snack bowls while he collected the juice boxes. Together, they walked into the kitchen.

Emotional tension sizzled between them. "I'm so sorry about the posters," Emma whispered, feeling she owed him that and much more, for the sticky situation they all found themselves in. She gripped his biceps and looked up at him seriously. "I didn't know what else to say...when they asked..."

His muscles tensed beneath her fingertips. "You know what they say," Tom said, gathering her close. "The heart wants what the heart wants."

Chapter Thirteen

And what he wanted, Tom thought, was Emma. Here with him. With his boys. Not just temporarily, either. But not sure she was ready to hear that just yet, given all she had going on, he contented himself with showing her how he felt instead. He lowered his head and kissed her tenderly until she melted against him.

Had they been alone, he would have taken her to bed. With the boys sleeping in the next room, that wasn't possible, so he let her go, promising himself he would finish what they had started the next time they were alone. Which would be soon, if he had anything to say about it...

Emma stepped back, lips glistening, eyes luminous.

"I can't even remember what we were talking about," she whispered.

Tom could. "The boys' All About My Family posters. The fact they wanted you included on them."

"Right." She squared her shoulders and moved away. Looking contrite again. "Which maybe wouldn't be so awkward if they had been more willing to put Vicki on them."

Tom didn't blame Emma for that.

"My guess is they don't want to talk about the fact that their mom is no longer here. At least not to a classroom full of their peers, who might ask uncomfortable questions."

Noting it would soon be dinnertime and this was the perfect time to get ready for that, while the boys were napping, he went into the garage and picked up the things he needed to start the grill and headed out back.

Emma and Buttercup tagged along with him.

"Of course, it could also be that I haven't done enough—aside from the photos they keep beside their beds—to keep Vicki real to them." He shrugged, filling the charcoal chimney with several sheets of paper on the bottom and then briquettes. "Or maybe they just need to move on. To a new, fuller life."

The way he was finally beginning to...

He also knew Vicki would approve. That she would want them all to find happiness again...

And there was no question, Emma brought them all joy. As did her dog, Buttercup.

Oblivious to the direction of his thoughts, Emma asked, "Do they have any memories of their mom?"

Tom shook his head, disappointed about that. "None that they haven't been told by me or Marjorie, and you can tell when they recite them, that parroting facts is all they are doing. There is no real emotional connection for them."

Cheeks flushed, she took a step toward him, looking more beautiful and impassioned than ever before. "You can't blame yourself for that, Tom."

He tore his eyes from the flowery spring dress she had on. The scoop neck bared her collarbones, and revealed the very uppermost swell of her soft breasts, curved in at all the right places, then fell in a swirl to just above her knees. "I should have taken more videos or at least shown the boys the ones that I have, more often," he admitted thickly.

"Why haven't you?"

His heart lurched. The familiar mixture of numbness and regret returned. "Initially, it was upsetting. Then they weren't interested. They didn't really seem to want to know anything about what their life with their mom had been like."

Emma closed the distance between them and took his hand in hers. She gazed down at their entwined fingers. "It doesn't mean they won't have questions, lots of them, later or want to know more about Vicki when they are older and can process it."

A shimmer of awareness, an undeniable bond, connected them. Glad the emotional intimacy was still there, stronger and more compelling than ever, he said, "You're very understanding."

Her eyes locked on his. Gentle now. Sympathetic. Taking him back to the time when they had been engaged. "I was in the same boat that they are now. Remember? I was only a little over a year old when my parents died in the house fire and roof collapse. Unlike my siblings, who all had different experiences in the foster homes they were sent to that night, I went straight to Carol and Robert's home, and was eventually adopted by them. I never felt the confusion and grief my siblings did. Which in itself brought on a whole lot of guilt. Because why was I so lucky, so bereft of suffering, when they weren't? Worse, I had no memories of my birth parents. And initially, quite honestly, was afraid to go there for fear I would get as upset as my siblings sometimes did over the loss."

Her vulnerability broke his heart. "Did that ever change?" He brought her closer still.

Emma stared up at him, thinking, considering. "To a point. But there is a part of me that still doesn't want to go there. I'd rather focus on the present, and keep moving on."

He studied the soft shimmer in her eyes. "I don't like to dwell in the past, either. Especially when it comes to the painful stuff," he rasped.

"So, we're agreed?" She placed her hand over his heart. "We should just let the boys feel what they feel and express what they want or need to express? Not that this is any of my business, of course," she added hastily. Looking suddenly fearful of interfering.

Aware how much she had taken on with his sons, he tenderly stroked his hand down her spine and said, "Of course it's your business," he told her resolutely. "We all appreciate the help you have given us."

She smiled. "Good to know…"

"Daddy...?" Austin asked plaintively from the doorway. "We waked up. The movie is broken."

Tom let go of Emma and turned to face his son. "I paused it so you wouldn't miss anything."

Crocket appeared, rubbing his eyes. "What are you doing?" He blinked at the smoke coming out of the charcoal chimney.

"Getting the grill ready to cook hotdogs and corn on the cob for dinner."

Bowie stifled a yawn. "Can we have some-mores, too?"

Tom nodded. "If you all eat your dinner, you sure can."

Luckily, it took almost zero persuasion to get them to eat their evening meal, and Emma stayed to help him get the boys in bed. "Are you going to be here in the morning when we wake up?" Austin asked, dropping his head onto his pillow.

"I like it when you sleep over," Bowie said.

"Me, too." Crockett snuggled deeper into his covers.

Tom found himself wishing for the same. Emma, however, had other ideas.

"You know how you all like sleeping in your own beds?" she asked the boys.

They nodded.

"Buttercup needs to be in her own bed tonight. And so do I."

"Can we come and see you tomorrow before school then?" Crockett pressed.

Fearing this was a little too much of an imposition, Tom interjected, "Guys, Emma has a really busy day tomorrow. She's giving the seniors at Laramie Gardens a tour of her studio."

"Actually, make that four tours." Emma went to each of the boys, adjusting their covers and kissing their temples in turn. Finished, she stood back. "But I'm never too busy for these guys. So sure, come on by and see us and if you get there with time to spare, I might even feed you a little before-school treat also known as breakfast."

"Were you serious about giving *four* tours?" Tom asked, as he walked her and Buttercup out to her SUV.

Aware how much this and every time she spent with Tom felt like a date that she never wanted to see end, Emma moved in a little closer to him. "Actually, so many people signed up we had to break them into groups. Seems like everyone wants to see firsthand how shoes are made."

"Or maybe they just enjoy spending time with you as much as I do."

"Well, there's that, which is mutual. But it's also a chance for me to practice my pitch on how shoes are made in my studio." Her lips curved into a fond smile. "The seniors aren't shy. They always have *lots* of questions. And will undoubtedly let me know if I am over- or underexplaining. Or repeating myself. Which means by the time I have to walk Barbara Roswald through the shoe-making process on Friday, I should have the whole pitch down pat."

He flashed her a look of approval. "You're really gearing up for this meeting, aren't you?"

"I am."

She was also scared to death.

So much was riding on this one meeting.

Too much?

Abruptly, she wondered if it was really her parents putting so much pressure on her. Or if she was the one actually doing it to herself...

"Hey, it's all going to be great. You'll see." Tom pulled her toward him for a long, thorough kiss that had her tingling from head to toe.

Slowly, they drew apart.

He threaded his fingers through her hair, lifting her face to his. "Text me when you-all get back to town so I know you made it home safely."

"I will," she promised, hugging him once more and getting into her car before she could think about the emotional implications.

They were supposed to be friends with temporary benefits, she reminded herself as she drove away. Yet they were acting more like a couple in love. And that was a big red flag.

They had been down that road once. Thinking love and/or passion would solve everything. Only to find themselves taking different paths in the end.

Tom's life was here in Laramie. Whereas she still had work ambitions to fulfill, which were likely to take her far away from Texas. So, as tempting as it was, they couldn't let themselves get too romantically entangled, never mind fall in love all over again. Not unless they knew for certain that she and Tom would be able to work things out now, the way they hadn't been able to in the past.

* * *

"Best information session ever!" Darrell Enloe proclaimed at four the next afternoon.

"I never knew so much labor went into each and every pair of shoes," Buck Franklin commented.

"Thank you so much for having us!" Miss Mim said.

"I can't wait until tomorrow's session!" Miss Patricia led the way out the door and onto the Laramie Gardens activity bus, at the same time Tom and his three boys approached.

"I'm looking forward to it, too." Emma winked at the group of mostly retired businessmen who had made up her last tour.

The bus departed.

Meanwhile, the triplets were looking around in awe. That morning, they had only been upstairs in her apartment. This was the first time they had seen the retail space, since it all had been put together. "It sure is pretty in here," Crockett said.

They admired the footwear on display.

"You have a lot of shoes!" Bowie observed.

Austin's brow furrowed. "But where are your glass slippers?"

Emma smiled. "I don't make those."

"But you're a princess lady!" Austin protested. "You have to have glass slippers!"

Buttercup ambled out of the workshop behind the showroom. Her tail wagged as she spotted the boys.

Before she could figure out how to respond, Tom held up the shopping bag they'd brought in with them and intervened. "Guys, why don't you take Buttercup in the other room, by her cushion, and show her the new toys we got?"

They excitedly went off. And were soon showing Buttercup her new pet toys.

When he was certain all was as it should be, Tom pivoted back to her. "Sorry. They're not usually so insistent when it comes to women's footwear."

Emma laughed at his droll tone. "Don't worry about it. Everyone's a critic. *Especially* today. But all the comments and questions I received gave me an awesome idea."

"Yeah? Do tell."

The sun streaming through the plate-glass windows caught the highlights in his dark brown hair, and she found herself basking in the perfection of his strong, chiseled jaw. Emma released a sigh. Despite the fact that she'd promised herself they would just be friends, deep down she was awfully glad to see him.

"Well, thanks to the residents of Laramie Gardens, I'm going to execute my first big focus group at the assisted living facility tomorrow."

Tom paused. "Is that your demographic?"

Good question. One she had yet to answer. "I don't know. I mean, I've always focused on the twenty- to thirty-year-old age group and my bestselling bridal boot. Hoping to earn a niche market."

As their eyes met and held, she felt a distinct shimmer of man-woman tension between them. He continued to study her with his steady amber gaze, as if trying to figure something out. "Which you seem to be doing."

Needing him on board with her ideas, for reasons she couldn't really comprehend, she continued seriously, "But maybe I've been unnecessarily limiting myself. Anyway, I'm going to listen to what the seniors have to say, and they've promised they will get any staff who would like to participate, most of whom are a lot younger, who are interested. Plus Ian Baker is going to talk to me about the financials, since he used to approve small business loans as part of his job before he retired."

"Nice."

"I know. It's amazing how helpful people are in Laramie County."

"Like everyone says. It's all about neighbor helping neighbor."

And Tom helping her.

The boys being around.

And Buttercup entering all their lives...

How was it her life had changed so much in so little time? And for the better?

She glanced into the other room, where the kids were still busy showing Buttercup how to play with her new dog toys. "Have you ever thought about getting the boys a puppy?"

Tom let out an affectionate laugh. "I think they've found one."

Unless, Emma thought anxiously, she and Buttercup left.

The same thought apparently occurred to Tom. He

ran the flat of his hand beneath his jaw. "Seriously, I didn't consider them old enough."

"But maybe they are?"

The triplets came back out into the showroom. As usual, Crockett took the lead. "Daddy, can we ask Princess Lady Emma now?"

Reluctance etched Tom's handsome face. "I told you boys. She is awfully busy this week."

Bowie looked on the verge of stomping his foot. "But this is important, Daddy!"

Apparently so. Emma knelt to square off with the triplets. "What is it, guys?"

Austin drew a deep breath. "We get to do presentations for our posters."

"And family gets to be there!" Bowie said excitedly.

"And we really, *really* want you to come!" Crockett declared.

Emma found she wanted that, too. She smiled. "When is it?"

The preschoolers looked at their dad. Tom said, "Wednesday morning, between nine and ten. In their different classrooms."

The boys began jumping up and down. Speaking all at once. "Can you, Princess Lady Emma? Please! It will be fun!"

Put that way? How could she refuse?

Unless…

She had to wonder. Did Tom want her there?

She pivoted to him. His expression was maddeningly inscrutable. Hoping they were on the same page about this as well, she drew a bolstering breath. "What do you think?"

"If you have time, it would be great," he said in a gravelly voice.

Maybe make up for the fact that they wouldn't have Vicki or Marjorie in attendance, his glance said.

Her mind made up, Emma turned back to The Alphabet Gang and hugged them all in turn. "It sounds *very* exciting. So yes," she told them with a great big smile, "I would be happy to come to your school to cheer you-all on."

Chapter Fourteen

"Hey Mom, what's up?" Emma asked the next morning.

"Just checking in," Carol said. "Your father and I haven't heard much from you since you moved into your new place."

Guilt flooded through her. She knew she had kept them out of the loop, but Laramie was a small town. Word spread fast. How much had gotten back to them?

"Everything is good," Emma said, still not wanting to tell them about the upcoming meeting with Ready to Wear Bridal at the end of the week. "I've been setting up the studio and my new apartment. Helping Tom with his triplets, while Marjorie is out of the country. And yesterday, I gave tours to the seniors from

Laramie Gardens and explained the process of making shoes and boots to them."

Carol's stamp of approval came through in her low, approving voice. "That's a lot."

"Plus I've been getting Buttercup acclimated to her new home." Emma petted her dog and was rewarded with a thumping tail and adoring look. "Speaking of whom, I was just heading out to take her to the groomer's to drop her off for a spa day." After which she was headed to Laramie Gardens to conduct her focus group.

"Can I do anything to help?" her mom asked.

"I think I've got it. But thanks for the offer."

Carol paused. "All right, I'll let you go then."

Picking up on the hint of sadness in her mom's voice, Emma promised, "Marjorie is coming back from Italy on Saturday, and Tom's going to Denver to pick her up. So maybe I can see you and Dad then." When she knew how the meeting with buyer Barbara Roswald had gone. "We can catch up."

"We'd like that," her mom said. "Until then, just know, your father and I are always here for you."

Which meant Carol knew something of what had been going on, Emma thought. But not having the time or energy to get into it at that moment, she signed off with her mom, and left to take Buttercup to the groomer's.

"Turnout was better than expected!" Emma's sister Faith observed four hours later.

She had come down from the LG financial services office to fill out a survey, too.

Emma smiled. Almost all the residents had come down to partake in the focus group. Employees had stopped by, too.

Faith picked up a clipboard and pen. "So how does this work?" she asked.

"Just answer the questions about all five styles of shoes and boots that are on display, and add any suggestions or comments at the end. And you don't have to put your name on it. In fact, it's probably better that you don't," Emma advised.

Miss Mim came up to join them. "The response has been overwhelmingly positive!" she declared.

Emma was happy about that, too. "Could be you-all just don't want to hurt my feelings," she declared.

"Well now, I wouldn't go so far as to say that," a deep masculine voice said from behind her.

Emma whirled to face the newcomer. "Tom!" She flushed despite herself. He looked so good in a sport coat, button-up shirt and jeans, his black Stetson slanted rakishly across his brow. He smelled incredible, too. Her heart pounded in her chest. "What are you doing here?"

He inclined his head at Miss Mim. "I got an SOS. Was told you were going to need help packing up."

Miss Isabelle lifted a staying palm. "You're going to have to give us your opinion first though," she said.

Emma wasn't sure, but she thought she saw a couple of the men wink at each other.

Ted Tarrant wheeled his chair to the front of the

group. His devoted wife, Tillie, was right behind him. "Which shoe or boot is your favorite?" he asked.

Miss Isabelle held up a clipboard. "Not to worry, Tom. I'll fill out your form for you."

Knowing they were really backing the poor guy into a corner, Emma stepped forward to rescue him. She cupped her hand around his biceps, felt the enticing swell of muscle beneath her fingertips. "I'm not sure we should put this cowboy on the spot."

At her save, Tom's broad shoulders relaxed ever so slightly. "I've never been an expert on ladies shoes," he told the fast growing group assembled around them.

"But surely you know what you like," Darrell Enloe persisted.

Emma sure did. *Tom!* Now where had that thought come from?

He inhaled. "Well, if I had to pick a favorite, it would be the wedding boot."

Miss Mim fanned herself, as if she were having a hot flash. Twinkling glances abounded.

"Any particular reason why?" Miss Patricia asked, taking the lead.

With an odd look, Tom conceded, "It's...ah... pretty?"

More grins, all around.

"What's *your* favorite, Emma?" Kurtis Kelley asked.

She didn't know what the seniors were working up to, but it was definitely something. She put her hands on her hips and tried to curtail the building orneriness. "You know I can't answer that!" she teased the seniors. "That's like asking a momma which of her babies she loves the best."

Everyone laughed, just as she had hoped.

"Well. Which is the best to dance in?" Miss Isabelle asked.

Emma squinted. Where in heaven's name were they going with this? "Actually, I...think they are all about the same."

Wilbur Barnes folded his arms across his barrel chest. "Well, I for one would like to see how those wedding boots look on a dancing bride."

A murmur of assent followed. "Maybe you could put on a pair and show us how they look," Russell Pierce said.

"Those boots are the right size, aren't they?" Nessie Rogers inquired.

Faith finished her survey, then piped up informatively. "Oh, not to worry. Emma makes all her sample shoes in her size."

"So, then they should fit like a dream," Miss Mim declared.

"I know it may seem silly to you, but we really want to see what those fancy boots look like in action," Ian Baker said.

The retired banker had been kind enough to go over the ins and outs of small business loan applications before she had gotten started.

She turned to Tom, hoping he would help bail her out.

He shrugged. "I sort of see their point."

Was he in on this, too?

No way to be sure. But there was definitely a feeling of building mischief in the dining hall.

"Plus," Tom continued, even more impishly, "it's always easier to judge apparel if it's on a pretty model."

"Aww," the seniors murmured.

Tillie Tarrant beamed. "He thinks she is pretty!"

"Because she is!" Buck Franklin said with a chuckle.

Emma cringed. This was fast getting out of hand.

Deciding the best way to get the conversation back on track was to get the attention back on the product she was trying to focus test, she sat down in a chair, slipped off her flats and laced up a pair of her top-selling wedding boots. Finished, she stood. The satin covering with the lace overlay covered her foot and hugged her leg to midcalf. The heel gave her another three inches in height.

"Those really would be perfect for a bride to wear on her wedding day," Tillie Tarrant observed sentimentally.

"Yeah. Her groom would love 'em, too," Tillie's husband, Ted, said.

Finding a way to divert the attention away from herself, Emma put in, "Actually, all my sisters wore them."

Miss Patricia tilted her head. "Weren't Emma and Tom engaged once?"

"Oh yes!" Miss Mim confirmed. "They were inseparable the entire time they were growing up, and dated all the way through high school and college!"

Only to break up and have Tom marry and have

children with someone else, Emma thought sadly, trying desperately to hang on to her remaining reserve.

Despite the fact that everyone around them already seemed to have them reunited and heading down the aisle!

"Well, they make a cute couple now!" Nessie Rogers winked.

Emma held up a staying hand. She did not dare look at Tom. She did not want to see what was in his eyes. "We're *not* a couple," she rushed to say. Even though it kind of felt like they were.

"Well, from what we've all heard, you-all sure have been spending a lot of time together recently," Miss Sadie said.

"Because Tom's mother is on vacation and he needed help with his boys," Emma protested. Heat rose in her chest. Was it hot in here, or what?

"Is that all it is…?" the ever-romantic Tillie Tarrant inquired, looking first at Emma, then Tom.

He kept his poker face as all eyes turned to him. "I can neither confirm nor deny…"

Chuckles broke out among the gathering crowd.

Without warning, Chris Young's "Heartbeat" began to play on someone's phone.

"…the way the light it hits your eyes…and makes me come alive…"

And just like that, Emma's heartbeat kicked up. She had to fight not to tap her foot to the rollicking song.

"…no mistaking…gets me every time…like some old roller coaster ride…"

The men looked at Tom, grinning encouragement.

Buck Franklin said, "It's not polite to leave a young lady waiting to be asked to dance, son."

The corners of Tom's eyes crinkled. "Good point." Before Emma could do more than draw a breath, he took her by the hand and brought her close.

The next thing she knew they were two-stepping to the music. Their bodies remembered how they used to move. As if they had never been apart.

The seniors were as thrilled by the lively display as she felt.

And in that moment, Emma realized their request had never been about the shoes.

It was about bringing her and Tom back together.

And darn it all, if a huge part of her heart didn't want that, too.

"I need to know something," Emma told Tom when they got back to her studio half an hour later. And had finished carrying in the surveys and travel trunk that held her sample shoes. "Why did you let them goad you into dancing with me?"

His grin turned as wide as all Texas. "The same reason I gave you a spin, dip and kiss at the end. I figured letting them feel their matchmaking was a success was the surest way to get the pranking to end."

She didn't know whether to stamp her foot indignantly, like one of his sons middrama, or kiss him wildly again. Trouble was, she wanted to do both. "So you knew…" she drawled, aware he could get under her skin like no other. Especially when he was trying to flirt with her…

"That they wanted sparks to fly between us? Yeah. I figured as much when I got the call to come over to Laramie Gardens."

She headed up the back stairs to her apartment. "You know they are going to be even more determined to get us back together now."

Tom followed her up to her apartment, looking as casually at home as if he lived there. He took his hat off and dropped it on a table. "You see that as a bad thing?"

Tipping her head back, she caught her breath. The erotic memory of dancing with him, hitting her full force again. "I…"

He caught her in his arms, held her when she would have run and brought her so close she could feel his hardness pressing against her. "Because I don't," he whispered against her mouth.

A friends-with-benefits arrangement was not what Tom wanted from Emma. Never had been, despite what he had allowed her to believe. It was also the surest way to make her see that the ties between them had never really been severed. Put in the deep freeze for a number of years, maybe, while they each went different ways. But, as far as he was concerned, these past couple of weeks had proven that their bond was stronger than ever.

Bottom line? At the end of the day, she was still the sweet and sassy, fiercely independent woman he had fallen in love with. A woman who had her whole life ahead of her. If only she would allow herself to put aside all their past hurts and disappointments and want more.

Appreciating the sweet, hot, sultry taste of her mouth, he ran a hand down her spine, lingering over her hips, lifting her, until she moaned at the onslaught of pleasure inundating them both.

"Tell me this doesn't feel right," he demanded, as she quivered again in response.

She released a quavering breath. "Of course, it does." She dug her fingers into his shoulders, kissed him back with a wantonness beyond his wildest dreams. She paused to look deep into his eyes. "We're human…"

And meant to be together. For more than just a few days or weeks…

If this was all he could get her to admit to now, then so be it.

Satisfaction roaring through him, he savored the taste and feel of her. Loving the way she rocked against him. The silky feel of her skin beneath his fingertips, as they undressed. The way she pulsed and melted against him when they hit the sheets. First shuddering with passion, then going hot and rigid with need. And most of all, he loved the way she let her self-control evaporate and all her inhibitions float away…

Even though she knew she might be fighting a losing battle, Emma wanted to keep things light and sexy between them. Concentrate on the moment, and the hard, hot body lying next to her. Which was not hard to do.

She kissed him feverishly, stroking his hard pecs

and hair-roughened thighs. Finding all the pleasure points of his big, warm body. Allowing him to find hers in return. Until he was all she wanted, all she needed.

He found protection. She watched as he rolled it on. Then he was sitting up against the headboard, dragging her upward to straddle his lap. Savoring the scent and feel of him, she wrapped her arms around him, pressing her breasts into the comforting warmth and hardness of his chest. And then there was nothing but the fusing of their bodies, the sense of being taken, loved, found. Nothing but the pleasure, the feeling of being truly and intimately connected to each other, once again.

Afterward, Emma snuggled against Tom until their breaths slowed. Then…it was back to the real world, as always. Reluctantly, Emma lifted her head and looked at the time on her cell phone. Nearly three thirty. Almost time for pre-K pickup. Wishing they could stay there for at least a little while longer, knowing they couldn't, she slid off his lap and eased from the bed.

Tom began to dress, too.

Her cell rang.

Emma looked at the screen. Saw it was Mimi Alexander, Barbara Roswald's assistant, calling. Immediately, she sobered. "I've got to get this."

Nodding, he moved soundlessly out of her bedroom.

She listened to the news. Stunned but accepting.

"Yes. It's fine. Right. Thanks for letting me know." She ended the call. Silence fell.

After a moment, Tom appeared in the doorway, looking strong and protective. "Everything okay?"

Aware she had to get a move on, too, if she were going to pick up Buttercup at the groomer's, she went to find the pink-floral leash, then her bag. She slid her cell phone into it. Pulled out her keys, still feeling a little shell-shocked. "My meeting with Barbara Roswald has been moved up. It's tomorrow at 1:00 p.m., instead of Friday."

Tom frowned at her kitchen sink, which was now dripping every couple of minutes, then turned back to her. "So you won't be able to make the boys' presentations tomorrow at the preschool." He walked over to test the handle. It was as tight as it could go.

Not wanting to mess with that now, Emma waved him toward the door. "I can do both. The event is from 9:00 to 10:00 a.m., right?"

Tom gave a last, lingering look at the plumbing issue. Then followed, apparently aware he had to go too, to pick up the boys at pre-K. He opened the apartment door for her. "With cookies and punch afterward, but yeah." He turned sideways as she passed. "It all should be over with by eleven at the latest."

Emma paused to lock up. "Well, then, I'll be there. Tonight is a different story, though." She made no effort to hide her disappointment. "I can't do dinner. I'm going to need the time to prep."

"I understand." They headed down the stairs together.

She cast a look over her shoulder. "Will the boys be okay with me canceling?"

"Yes," Tom said firmly.

And though she knew he could handle his boys, even when they were difficult, massive guilt flowed through her anyway. Was this the way working moms felt? Torn between family and career? Fearful of disappointing everyone?

He was looking at her, weighing something. She wasn't sure what. She didn't like the feeling they weren't exactly on the same page anymore. "You're sure?" It was ironic. She had waited years to have an opportunity like this, but right now all she could think about were those three little faces. Not what Ready To Wear Bridal might or might not offer.

He wrapped a reassuring arm about her shoulders. Leaning down, he pressed a kiss on the top of her head. "I'm positive, sweetheart. My mom is coming back Saturday. Mother's Day is Sunday, and I need to do some errands in San Angelo in advance of those events. I'll just take them with me."

He kept his arm around her as they walked out. Finally releasing her when they reached their vehicles, which were parked side by side. "*Errands?* Yikes. Now you really have me worried," she teased. Given that it was the triplets' antics in the grocery store that had gotten them spending so much time together again.

He chuckled. "Not to worry, Princess Lady Emma," he told her in the low, gruff sexy voice she loved. "I've got this." He wrapped both arms around her waist and brought in her close. Kissing her again, in public, for the second time that day. "Just like you've got your big pitch tomorrow..."

He was so confident, she thought, as she looked into his eyes. She couldn't help but be, too.

Chapter Fifteen

"We have a bit of a crisis going on," Tom said the next morning when he came to pick her up for the boys' family presentations.

A little nervous herself about her own presentation later in the day, Emma followed him out to his pickup truck. "Oh no. What happened?"

Tom opened the door for her, then circled around to climb inside. He started the engine, then looked over his shoulder and pulled out into the morning traffic. Large capable hands circling the wheel, he explained, "I had a call, shortly after I dropped the boys off this morning. They told their teachers that because they made their posters together, they had to talk about them together."

Emma shifted in her seat to better see his face. "But

they are in different classes now, and each child is supposed to present only to their classmates and guests."

"Exactly." He frowned, as they neared the preschool, and he saw all the parents currently looking for a place to park. Because the lot was full, he drove on down the street to the residential area where street parking was allowed. He steered into the first available space, being careful not to obstruct the homeowner's mailbox or driveway. "But that did not deter The Alphabet Gang." He got out and came around again to help her with her door.

Tom held out a hand as she stepped down, her heels sinking into the soft grass. Then escorted her onto the sidewalk, continuing his tale of woe.

"The boys insisted they had to do it together or not at all."

Emma could see that. Especially since the story of their "family" contained emotional elements they could potentially find difficult to discuss.

He moved in closer, keeping his voice low, as they proceeded toward the preschool. "Fearing a meltdown of epic proportions about to ensue, that could set off an ensuing wave among all the students, the school's director came up with a solution." As he leaned in close, she saw how closely he had shaved and caught a whiff of his cologne. "So now, the boys will present together, at ten thirty, in the school cafeteria, right before the celebratory cookies and juice are served."

It was all she could do not to take his hand and squeeze it hard. But not sure if that was appropriate in this situation, she merely remained close as they navigated their way through the packed parking lot and other parents heading into the school. "Do you think it will bother them to have triple the crowd listening to them?"

Tom squinted down at her, appearing as if he wanted to embrace her, too. The corners of his lips twisted. "Hard to tell. They've never had stage fright before. Usually, when they are together, they are like the three musketeers." He cupped her elbow, assisting her as she stepped from the pavement onto the concrete sidewalk.

Her arm tingled from his gallant touch, even after he let go.

"Feeling the strength in their camaraderie…" he added.

They waited for another group of eager parents to go on ahead. She smiled up at him. "Well, hopefully the same will be true today."

"Also—" Tom paused, just before they walked in the door "—I should warn you. They made some last-minute additions to their posters before they left for school today, too."

Uh-oh. Was this part of the reason for the near meltdown? "Good ones?" she asked nervously.

Tom inhaled, but, to her frustration, did not elaborate further. He reached over and briefly squeezed her hand. "I hope."

Tom and Emma sat through some of the presentations in the other three preschool classes, just as they would have had the morning gone off without a hitch.

Then, toward the end, they escorted the boys down to the lunchroom where the reception was to be held.

One of the aides was already on the stage. She had three easels, each one bearing a poster from one of Tom's sons. She talked to the Reid boys about what was going to ensue, while Emma and Tom took a seat at one of the tables near the front.

The rest of the classes and parents filed in. Finally, it was showtime.

Kelly Shackleford-McCabe, one of the teachers, explained that the boys were going to be doing their talks together. A few of the parents looked mystified. But most knew that the boys had lost their mom two years before and might be having difficulty with this assignment.

The kids were more curious than concerned about the change in parameters.

"Would you like to tell us about this person?" Kelly asked, pointing at Tom's photo near the top.

"This is our daddy. He's a cowboy," Crockett said.

"He's great at riding horses, and moving cattle, but he can't cook very good," Bowie said, nodding.

"And he has buildings in town he has to take care of, too. Which is why he doesn't have time to make real waffles for us, only the ones that go in the toaster," Austin concluded.

Beside her, Emma could see Tom struggling not to wince at that last part.

"Who is this?" Kelly pointed at Marjorie.

"That's our gramma," Austin said. "She talks a lot and she is *very patient*, which she says, is a really good thing. She is in Italy now on a vacation. She calls us every day because she says she has to check up on us."

Bowie pointed to the Marjorie on his poster. "Gramma said Daddy couldn't take care of us by himself, that he needed a woman, which is why Princess Lady Emma has to help out. A lot."

Crockett added enthusiastically, "Princess Lady Emma knows how to make waffles 'from scratch,' and hers are much better than the ones daddy makes, even when he uses his special tricks like putting them in the toaster twice."

"Wow." Kelly nodded, taking it all in. "And who are these three guys?" She pointed to the photos of the triplets.

"That's us," Crockett crowed proudly.

"We're The Alphabet Gang, 'cause our names start with *A*, *B* and *C*," Bowie said.

"And we're triplets, which means we were all born at the same time. And are the same age, and everything." Austin concluded.

"Are there any differences between you?" Kelly asked.

This stumped them.

Finally, they shook their heads.

Which was maybe, Emma thought, why the teachers had wanted them to be in separate classrooms, so they would have a stronger sense of individual self.

Next, Kelly pointed at the photo of Buttercup. "Who is this?"

"Her name is Buttercup," Bowie said. "She's an

Australian labradoodle that belongs to Princess Lady Emma."

"But she comes to our ranch *a lot*, since Gramma left," Crockett explained.

"And she stays over sometimes, too," Austin added, "which means we can play with her in the morning before school."

"Very nice." Kelly urged them on. Sensing they were in potentially embarrassing territory, she pointed to the photo of Emma. "And this is…?"

"Princess Lady Emma." Crockett grinned. "She's our daddy's friend. And she is very nice."

"She's a real good cook, too," Austin added. "'Cause she makes breakfast for dinner whenever we ask her if we can have that."

"But," Bowie said, sighing, "she doesn't have any glass slippers, which is sad, because she is a princess and princesses are supposed to have glass slippers, otherwise they won't kiss their prince. So—" he drew a big breath, as if about to launch into a very important, very detailed tale of woe "—we told daddy…" Abruptly, Tom caught Kelly's eye. He made the time-out sign.

She stepped in, to cut off whatever it was Bowie had been about to divulge.

Emma suspected it was about some private conversation they'd previously had with Tom.

"And the last thing on your posters is all a little different," Kelly observed with a smile, looking at the late additions. Which at first glance didn't seem to relate. "Austin has drawn…?"

"An angel, with wings and a halo," Austin explained.

"Crockett...?"

"That's the sky, with clouds. Which is where heaven is."

Emma's heart caught in her chest. "And Bowie," Kelly continued gently, "you have a photograph?"

"Yes, that's Vicki," Bowie said with pride, exuding none of the sadness Emma—and pretty much everyone in the audience who had known her—was feeling. "She's our mom. She died when we were two years old. She lives in heaven now."

The audience was so silent you could hear a pin drop. Here and there Emma saw tears glistening. She didn't dare look at Tom, because they were in her eyes, too.

"We can't see her anymore," Crockett reported, "except in the pictures we keep by our beds."

"But we talk to her every night when we say our prayers with Daddy," Austin said.

Bowie added brightly, "And we blow a kiss at her picture, too. Just the way she taught us."

"That must be very comforting," Kelly said, looking as if she were suddenly struggling not to burst into empathetic tears herself.

The triplets angled their heads at her.

Austin stepped up to pat Kelly's hand reassuringly. "It's okay," he said as Bowie patted her other hand. "We're getting a new mom now," he explained.

Crockett turned to the audience and pointed, adding firmly, "That's her. Princess Lady Emma!"

* * *

Tom had thought he dodged a bullet when Kelly had kept the boys from revealing their glass slipper plan. But that was nothing compared to the realization that his three boys now considered Emma to be their new-mom-in-waiting.

As the audience started to clap in appreciation, Emma turned to him, whispering in his ear. "I am so sorry," she whispered, looking mortified by the assumption. Whether because the boys had come up with the idea on their own, or she just did not want to even be in the running for their new mom, he could not say.

Maybe it was all just too much too soon, as her older brother Travis seemed to worry. Especially when she had the biggest opportunity of her career ahead of her this afternoon.

Figuring they could talk about it later, he leaned in close and murmured low, so only she could hear, "Don't worry about it. No one cares what was just said."

Her brow lifted, intimating this was going to be all over the Laramie grapevine in no time. And his mother and her family would likely hear about it, and come to their own erroneous conclusions, too. Forcing them to explain things they could barely get a handle on themselves. Like exactly where their relationship was headed.

All he knew for sure was that she'd managed to re-suscitate his heart, and he didn't want to go back to the way things were before she came back into his life.

Any more than he wanted their time together to end when his mother returned on Saturday, and could take over much of the care of the kids again.

And he had thought—hoped—she was beginning to feel the same way.

Noticing she still looked worried about what had been revealed about their recent interactions, Tom leaned even closer, as the clapping died down and finally ended. "Kids are notoriously givers of too much information. I am sure everyone here has already forgotten all about the things they blurted out."

Emma gazed around, watching as the parents and preschoolers reunited and began heading for the big tables set up with the celebratory cookie and juice-box buffet. "I guess you're right," she murmured back, relaxing slightly.

Crockett, Bowie and Austin dashed up to join them. "Did you like our presentation?" Austin asked.

Crockett and Bowie waited anxiously, too.

The woman they wished would be their new mom did not disappoint. "I did!" Emma said joyously, hugging them all in turn. "You all did *such* a good job, telling about your family."

"Except," Bowie said with a frown, "we didn't get to finish about the shoes..."

And a good thing, too, Tom thought fervently. He lifted a hand, promising, "That's okay. We can always talk about it later when we get back to the ranch after school."

Unconvinced, Crockett turned to Emma. "Do you like shoes that have lights in them?"

Her expression baffled, she glanced down at their shoes. "You mean like your sneakers?" she asked, pointing to the flashing safety lights embedded in the fabric and soles that lit every time they moved.

Bowie shook his head, correcting her. "These are for kids, Princess Lady Emma. We mean for grown-ups."

Austin drew a big breath. "Like..."

"...the ones we saw last year when Grandma and I took you to Disney World," Tom cut in to help his sons explain. Before they once again relayed far too much. "And we watched the Electric Light Parade. And went to see some of the musical shows, like the one for Cinderella. The Disney characters had all sorts of fancy costumes, didn't they, guys?"

The boys nodded enthusiastically. Eager to share the experience with Emma, they launched into stories of everything they had seen and done on their trip to Florida. They were still talking about the Magic Kingdom and the safari ride in the animal park, as they went through the line, and then sat together and ate their treats.

Soon, it was time for them to head out to an early recess, which today was being held before instead of after lunch.

"Bye Princess Lady Emma!" the boys chorused, giving her a hug.

"Bye, Alphabet Gang!" Emma returned, embracing them back.

The boys giggled at her gentle teasing and hugged their dad. Emma and Tom watched as they ran over to get in the lines of their various teachers, then headed out. And it was only then that Emma glanced at the time on her phone.

Chapter Sixteen

"Oh no," Emma said, noting it was nearly eleven forty, and her big meeting was scheduled for one o'clock! She had been so enthralled, spending time with Tom and the boys, she had completely lost track of time.

"What can I do to help?" Tom asked.

She walked faster out of the preschool parking lot. "I need to pick up a box of tea sandwiches from The Cowgirl Chef, tea cakes from the Sugar Love Bakery. Both should be ready. But with the lunch rush starting…" How long would it take?

"No problem." He took her hand in his. Tingles spread outward, through not just her arm, but her entire body. "I'll get both for you."

Resisting the urge to throw herself into his arms

for a brief, reassuring hug, she contented herself with giving him a grateful smile, instead. "Thank you!"

The day suddenly began to seem as if it were getting unbearably warm. The casual affection in his eyes deepened. As they continued to move in perfect harmony toward the residential street where he had parked, he gave her lips a long, thorough once-over. "What else?"

Feeling suddenly unbearably restless, she picked up the pace even more, her heels clicking purposefully on the concrete sidewalk. "My studio is all set up, but I need to put the linens on the table in the apartment. Change clothes. Probably touch up my makeup and hair."

He flashed another gentle, protective smile. "What about Buttercup?"

"My sister-in-law Susannah picked her up this morning. She's going to stay there and hang out with Susannah's golden retriever, Daisy, until my business is concluded."

Tom unlocked the passenger door and helped her make the step up into the cab. Never the easiest thing to do in a skirt.

He climbed behind the wheel, started the engine with a press of a button, and eased out of the space onto the street. "Smart." All business mode now, he asked, "What else do you need?"

Emma consulted the list on her cell phone. "A bouquet from the florist, for the table."

Tom took a shortcut that bypassed the traffic leaving the preschool. And headed toward downtown. "Any flowers in particular?"

Emma drew a deep enervating breath, realizing too late she should have preordered this, too. Would have, had she not been in such a tizzy trying to get organized for her big meeting. Two whole days early! She sent Tom a look, aware how nice it was to be able to lean on him this way.

When they had been together before, they had been a couple, but still planted firmly on their own paths. Now, it felt like they were a team. The kind that made a strong, loving family...

Oblivious to her thoughts, Tom was still listening, waiting.

Forcing herself to get back on task, she said, "Whatever they have ready to go that would be appropriate for an early- to mid-afternoon tea is fine."

He put on his signal and turned onto Main Street, heading for their destination. "I never knew you for a tea person."

Emma gulped around the tightness in her throat. "I'm not really. But Barbara Roswald is. And since she didn't have time for a lunch or dinner, her assistant Mimi Alexander, suggested that I might do this..."

He pulled up to the curb in front of The Boot Lab. "I'll hit the three shops and be back as soon as I can."

"Thank you." On impulse, she leaned over to kiss his cheek, feeling so glad he was back in her life. Even if they hadn't yet figured out how it was all going to work out. She only knew she wanted it to, so much. She smiled and kissed him again, squeezing his biceps. "You're a lifesaver."

Emma'd had her wardrobe crisis the evening before, finally settling on a simple sky blue sheath, and a pair of her business pumps in a geometric sky and marine blue designed leather.

Quickly, she traded out the skirt and blouse she'd worn to the preschool and freshened her hair and makeup.

Taking a deep breath, she spread out the linens on her café table and set out the china that she had borrowed from her sister-in-law Allison.

She was just about to fill the electric teakettle when footsteps sounded on the stairs. Followed by a knock.

"Come in!" she yelled, then realizing he might need some help, set the kettle down and rushed over to the portal.

He swung open the door with one hand. The two boxes and flowers were held by his other palm, against his chest. In that instant, he was every bit the gallant hero. Sexy and handsome enough to grace any fairy tale. She could see why the boys, who already thought she was a princess, believed they belonged together...

In her heart she felt so, too.

The only question was how...

Not that this needed to be answered today.

His gaze drifted over her, taking her in. Deepening affection lit his golden brown eyes. "You look magnificent."

She had needed to hear that. So much. She smiled back at him. "Thank you."

He looked down at the things in his hands, swiftly getting them back on task. "I didn't know if you had a vase, so I just asked the florist to go ahead and put the bouquet in one. Hope that is okay."

"It's great."

Aware her heart was racing, and not just in anticipation of the biggest business opportunity of her entire life, Emma filled the delicate china platters, which were also from Allison, covered them with plastic wrap and set them in the fridge. She turned back to Tom.

"What else can I do?" he asked softly, looking as if he wanted to make love with her as much as she wanted to make love to him.

A thrill went through her.

She drew a breath. "I think I've got it."

Realizing she still needed to put the kettle on, she went back to the sink. Turned the dripping spigot, a little more quickly than usual. Then let out a startled cry when the entire thing came off in her hand.

Cold water sprayed upward, hitting her in the chest and face.

Tom sprang into action, shifting her aside and dropping down to his knees. He opened the cabinet door, reached inside and shut the water off.

Too late.

Water was everywhere. The front of Emma's dress and her bangs were drenched. And that was, of course, when the buzzer sounded.

An exceedingly polite male voice came out of the speaker. "This is Ralph Young. Ms. Roswald's driver for the day. Just wanted to let you know her car is out front."

Emma gulped, and did her best to sound composed. "Thank you."

The voice on the other end of the intercom continued, "She's on a call now. She'll let you know when she can come in."

"That's fine. Thank you!" Emma said. She swung around so fast, she bumped into Tom's hard chest. This was a freaking disaster! "What are we going to do?" she asked in complete panic.

If she had only let him fix that sink earlier when he wanted to...

Hand to her shoulder, he steered her toward her bedroom. As calm as she was distraught. "Go dry off and change. I'll mop up here and go down to charmingly waylay Ms. Roswald if she is ready to come in before you are prepared to greet her."

Relief flowed through her. And just like that, Emma's sense of humor returned, easing her tension. Already moving toward her bedroom, she slanted a grateful look over her shoulder and quipped, "You're *charming*?"

Already in the midst of dropping down with a roll of paper towels to dry the floor, he chuckled. "As every prince should be." Finished, he rose and began mopping up the counters and sink. "Just ask The Alphabet Gang," he said with a wink. "They'll tell you."

* * *

Emma blotted the moisture from her face and ran a blow dryer through her bangs, then ditched her damp sheath for a three-quarter sleeved marine blue dress that would set off her shoes almost as well.

Pausing only long enough to draw a deep breath, she headed downstairs. Tom was already in the show-room, regaling Barbara Roswald with the details of the Laramie, Texas, historic district.

She seemed interested.

Tom turned and gave Emma a "you've got this" look only she could see. He smiled. "Here she is. I'll be on my way. And again, Ms. Lockhart, sorry I didn't get to that issue with the sink sooner."

Not sure how much he'd told the elegant-looking businesswoman, Emma merely nodded understand-ingly. "It's all good now."

Still smiling, Tom eased out the door.

Noticing a limo with a uniformed driver parked out front, Emma turned back to her guest. The buyer for the Ready To Wear Bridal chain was wearing a sleek black business suit and expensive gold jewelry. Her dark hair was drawn back into a knot at the nape of her neck, and her shoes were Jimmy Choo.

Emma knew she had her work cut out for her.

"Where would you like to start…?" she asked.

Tom spent the next few hours fielding an unex-pected series of phone calls, doing errands, and pick-ing up the boys at school and taking them to their "impromptu" playdate.

Every time he passed The Boot Lab, the limo was still parked out in front. Hoping that meant Emma's meeting was going well, he found a few more tasks to do in town.

Finally, around five thirty, Barbara Roswald came out and the limo drove off. He texted Emma to let her know he was outside, and she told him to come on up.

She let him in the door to her apartment, a smile plastered on her face.

Her face fell a little. "Where are the boys?"

He realized she thought he had the triplets with him. Had the smile really been for them? He pushed aside his disappointment. He wanted her to love his kids, and she clearly did. But he also wanted her to be equally attached to him. Trying not to wonder if he were second place in her heart, he responded to her questioning look and said, "Playdate."

Her shoulders slumped slightly. "Oh."

So she did want to see the boys. He followed her inside the apartment. Even more curious now. "How did it go with Barbara Roswald?"

"Honestly?" She disappeared into the bedroom, leaving the door slightly ajar. When she came back out, she had put on a pair of jeans and was pulling a striped navy and cream T-shirt over her head. "I don't have a clue."

"She was here a long time."

Emma looked around, considered a pair of custom western boots from Monroe's Western Wear, then finally put on a pair of sneakers. A new wave of color highlighted her cheeks. "Surveilling me?"

Able to see her emotions were high, and she was struggling to contain them, he decided right then and there that if she needed him to be her soft place to fall, he would be that for her. "Staying close by in case there was another flood or something," he corrected her.

Emma ran her hands through her hair, then slipped back into the bathroom. When she returned, she had one of her clips in hand. "Well, thank goodness there wasn't." She twisted her chestnut locks into a knot, and then secured it on the back of her head. A few tendrils escaped, framing her face and the nape of her neck.

Damn, she was sexy, even when she wasn't trying to be.

He looked around. "You had tea together?"

Emma began clearing plates. She carried them to the sink, then as if remembering the faucet no longer worked, she stacked them in there anyway. "Yeah, I filled the tea kettle with filtered water from the bottle in the fridge. And Barbara seemed to enjoy it. I'll have to thank her assistant, Mimi, for suggesting it."

Emma turned back to face him. She lounged against the kitchen counter, bracing her hands on either side of her, and inhaled deeply. Her eyes met his. "And I should thank you too for all the charts and graphs you put together for me." Something else glimmered in her gaze he couldn't quite identify.

"Barbara was impressed by the way all the financial data was compiled," she added. "She said usually artistic types, like clothing and shoe designers, aren't good at the numbers side of things."

Emma was good at everything she tried. She just

didn't know it yet. Tom took up a place beside her. Elbowing her lightly, he sent her a sidelong glance. "Which is why you have me..."

Her eyes grew luminous. It was as if he had said something that touched her and worried her simultaneously.

Had something else happened?

"What did she think about your shoe designs?" Tom asked.

Emma shook her head in a way that indicated an unsettling uncertainty. "She came down here specifically to see the wedding boot, but she also looked at everything I've done to date. And took the portfolio, the financial prospectus you put together for me, as well as a few samples of the wedding boot, in all its different iterations, back with her, so she could show the team at headquarters in Chicago."

He turned toward her. "But no promises of doing business together yet?"

Emma pivoted toward him, too. "She has to talk to her colleagues. See what they think. If everyone wants to proceed, *and it has to be everyone*, they will let me know what the next steps are."

Knowing the wait had to be excruciating for her, given how much she had riding on it, he asked quietly, "Any timetable for that?"

Another worried sigh. "She hoped by the end of this week."

Two days.

"But," Emma added, biting her lip, "she wasn't making any promises."

"Well—" he tried to find the silver lining that would make Emma feel better "—that's good."

She put up a hand, interrupting him before he could say anything else. "Would you mind if we didn't talk about this anymore?" She sent him a brief, harried glance. "I have to go over to Susannah and Gabe's and pick up Buttercup."

Hopefully, her dog would help ease her stress. Not wanting to desert her in her time of need, though, especially when he knew he had another important task to complete, too, one he couldn't yet tell her about, Tom fell into step beside her. "Want me to go with you?"

She found her keys and phone, and tucked them into her shoulder bag. "Don't you have to get the boys?"

"Their playdate includes dinner." He touched the middle of her back, gently escorting her out the door, down the stairs. "Which means you and I could have supper…"

"Oh… I don't know."

Being by herself, burying all her angst deep inside, would not help her right now. Tom knew. Because that was what the two of them had both done whenever they reached a glitch in the road when they were together before. The self-imposed isolation was what had driven them apart. He didn't want to see it happen again. "Just think about it while I drive you over there."

Emma nodded. Briefly, she let herself lean into his touch. "Okay."

Unable to help but note how completely wiped out she looked, Tom drove across town, his heart going out to her. It was a good thing she didn't know what else lay ahead of her that evening.

Not that he could warn her.

When they got out of his truck, they found a note taped to the front door. It said:

Emma,
Had a bit of an emergency family thing. Butter-
cup is at the Circle L Ranch with your folks. I'll
explain later...
XOXO, Susannah

The news was apparently too much, he noted, his heart aching with compassion for her all the more.

Emma's slender shoulders sagged. She buried her face in her hands. "Oh my gosh, Tom! The last thing I need now is the third degree from my folks."

He paused, not sure what was really going on with her family, either. At least not all of them. What he did know was that they were a close-knit, protective, loving bunch who didn't hesitate to interfere in each other's lives if they thought action was needed. "I thought you weren't going to tell your folks about the meeting with RTW Bridal today?"

Emma blew out a gusty breath. "I didn't. But my mom knows something is up. She called me, fishing for information yesterday morning. I was able to beg off, because I was just leaving to take Buttercup to the groomer's and I know she was headed into work herself. But there will be no such saving graces this time to help me avoid her questions. Unless..." She spun to face him, need in her eyes. "Do you have time to drive out there with me?"

"You want me to go?" He hadn't been out to her family's ranch since they broke up. If she were open to taking him with her, in what she knew others would see as a public commitment of their renewed friendship, and/or possibly something more...then it meant her attitude about their future was changing, too.

And that could not be anything but a very good sign.

Oblivious of his fast-escalating feelings for her, her head bobbed in determination. "You can dominate the conversation and run interference for me. And then we'll say we have to run because of the boys..."

Actually, that excuse wasn't going to work, Tom thought. Emma would find out why soon enough. He wrapped an arm about her shoulders. "Sounds like a plan." The sooner they got this over with, the better. "Let's go..."

Emma hadn't let herself lean on any one person in years. Her siblings had always been there for her. Her parents, too. And the Rossi family in Italy.

But the only time she had let herself depend on just one person for most everything she needed in the way of physical, emotional and moral support, was when she and Tom had been together.

She had been there for him in the exact same way. Most of the time. The way she guessed most happily married couples were for each other.

Which meant that when they had broken up, the

gaping hole in her heart and her life had been unbearable.

She had not known where to turn.

How to cope.

How not to feel so lonely her heart ached.

Once she had picked herself up and put herself back together though, she had realized not only could she soldier on alone, but that she was much stronger and much more independent than she thought.

And with that strength and independence came an autonomy and freedom she had cherished.

She still liked knowing she could do things alone.

But she liked leaning on him, too.

Maybe more than she should…?

She sighed, more loudly than she intended.

Tom cast a glance at her, misunderstanding the reason for her loud exhalation of breath. "Almost there."

Another mile, she knew.

He slowed as he reached the tall, black metal archway that announced the entrance to the Circle L Ranch. "Thanks for driving me," Emma said, wishing she didn't have to keep her parents in the dark.

But if she told them about the meeting, they would overreact, so…

Tom nodded, suddenly looking no more eager for the confab than she was. And the moment they walked in the front door of the ranch house, and everyone jumped out and yelled, *"Surprise!"* she knew why.

Chapter Seventeen

"We're so proud of you!" Carol Lockhart embraced Emma with maternal affection.

"We knew this day would come!" her dad agreed.

Emma flushed to the roots of her hair. She stepped back, her gaze surveying her siblings and their spouses, and children. Tom's three sons were there, too.

She looked like she wanted to sink through the floor. Too late, he realized he should have found a way to delay this party until there really was something to celebrate.

"So what kind of deal are you getting with Ready To Wear Bridal?" her brother Noah asked. His three daughters, three-year-old twins and their eight-year-old sister, stayed close to him. Emma had told him the girls had been struggling since their move from

California to be closer to family. It still seemed to be the case. His heart went out to them. Losing a parent-slash-spouse was hard.

It could take years to be able to really move on, the way he and his boys were finally doing now.

"How did you know about that?" Emma asked Noah. She turned, slanting Tom a faintly accusing glance.

He shook his head slightly, letting her know, *It wasn't me.*

Carol waved her hand airily. "Oh, honey, there are no secrets in Laramie County!" she said, as Emma turned back to her folks. "You know that!"

"Not that it was easy for us to put it all together," her dad said. "But when the head buyer's personal driver went into The Cowgirl Chef to kill time, while he was waiting for his boss, and told Sage who he worked for...everyone kind of knew your time had finally come."

Emma swallowed. "That's the thing," she said, stepping back, closer to Tom. Sensing she needed his support, he slid his arm around her waist. "There is no deal yet, and there might not ever be."

"Doesn't matter," her dad said firmly, popping the champagne. "You're a huge success in all our eyes. And that's what matters..."

Maybe not to Emma, though, Tom thought, as she went cold in his embrace. She wanted validation of the most concrete kind.

"Your new design studio is getting rave reviews,

and you haven't even formally opened yet!" Carol handed Emma a glass.

"Everyone is very excited," Allison, a famous lifestyle blogger in her own right, said.

"As soon as you open you will be getting orders nonstop," her sister Mackenzie agreed.

"And then…" Crockett sidled up to Emma, eager to be heard too. He tipped his head up at her, beaming hopefully. "Maybe you will finally get some glass slippers!"

"With lights in them!" Austin agreed.

"And your *prince*, who will kiss you," Bowie said. "So you can live happily-ever-after!"

Everyone chuckled.

Emma looked touched by his sons' concern for her welfare. As well as embarrassed to have their hopes put out there that way.

What she didn't know, Tom thought, was that his emotions ran along the same lines as his three sons.

He stepped in to rescue her. "In case anyone can't tell," he said dryly, "my sons are very enthralled by the Cinderella story. Just like their grandmother, Marjorie."

"What's 'nthralled, Daddy?" Austin's brow furrowed.

"It means you like something or someone a lot," Tom said.

The triplets lit up. "We like Princess Lady Emma," Crockett confessed.

"A lot," Bowie agreed.

"And we love her, too," Austin said vehemently.

Emma blushed all the more. There were smiles all around. Her dad lifted a glass. "To Emma, and her amazing success!"

Because it was a school night, and all Carol and Robert's grandkids were in attendance, dinner came soon after. By seven thirty, the young ones were all yawning, or starting to get cranky with fatigue.

Emma looked at Tom, as if to say "get me out of here, please." He happily consented to her wishes. Gathering up his kids while she leashed Buttercup, he thanked Carol and Robert and said good-night to everyone. He waited until they were driving down the long Circle L Ranch drive, toward the two-lane country highway, before he asked, "Want me to take you back to town now?"

She started to nod, then glanced over her shoulder. Her expression turned tender. "I was going to say yes, but…" She inclined her head. "Look…" He glanced in his rearview mirror at the back seat. All three were already asleep.

"I think we better get them home and in bed ASAP."

We. He liked the way that sounded. The easy way she put the children's needs ahead of their own at times like this.

Still, he had to ask, "You sure?" She'd had a very long day, too. More business ahead if things worked out the way she no doubt wanted.

She nodded, her own fatigue beginning to show. "Positive."

Emma and Buttercup stayed with the vehicle, in

case anyone woke up, while Tom carried his sons up to bed, one at a time. Once there, he took off their shoes and put the covers over them. Then came back downstairs.

Emma was just bringing Buttercup in.

She also had all three school backpacks, which contained their lunch boxes and any important papers.

She set them in the kitchen.

"What can I get you?" he asked, as he opened the lunch boxes and wiped them out.

"A sparkling water."

"Coming right up." He pulled two from the fridge. Their hands touched as he passed one to her. "Listen, about the party tonight..."

The quiet misery he had evidenced earlier was back. She held up a hand, stop sign fashion. "I really don't want to talk about it, Tom." She turned on her heel and left the kitchen.

He let her go.

She obviously needed a minute.

He would give her that, then try again.

Unfortunately, when he went into the living room fifteen minutes later, she was already curled up on the sofa. Buttercup beside her. Both were sound asleep.

Figuring their talk could wait until the next day, he covered her with a blanket, bent and kissed her forehead, then went back to the kitchen to make the next day's lunches.

Hours later, the sound of thundering sneakers on the stair treads jolted Emma awake. She bolted upright.

"I told you she would be here!" Crockett exclaimed, as they rounded the corner and came into the formal living room.

"Yeah, but she still needs her glass slippers!" Bowie said.

"Guys!" Tom's voice cut through the chaos. Instantly, like a game of Statue, everything stopped.

"I told you," he said much more quietly. "We're running late today. You-all have to wash your face, brush your teeth and comb your hair before breakfast. So go!" He pointed to the stairs.

"And then we get to eat?" Austin asked.

"When we all get to town," Tom promised. "We will hit the drive-through window and get egg, bacon and cheese sandwiches and orange juice. You can eat it in the car before I take you in to school."

He turned to Emma, looking a bit frazzled. "Sorry. We all overslept."

She glanced at her watch and saw it was 8:15! "Give me five and Buttercup and I will be ready to go."

It was another ten minutes before they were all in the pickup truck. The boys snug in their safety seats, Buttercup snuggled in the roomy well at Emma's feet.

"Do you want anything?" he asked, as he pulled up at the fast food restaurant.

Emma shook her head. "But if you could drop me and Buttercup *before* you take the boys to school…" She had so much to do. And she had to be available for any calls from RTW Bridal.

He gave her the same look of understanding and

support he had evidenced since he had been back in her life. "No problem," he said.

And minutes later, he did just that.

Tom got a text from the post office saying he had a package for pickup, as he and the boys were finishing eating. Grabbing the box of wet wipes he kept in the truck, he got out and went around to open up the rear passenger doors.

"Do we get to see Emma after school?" Crockett asked. He lifted his face and held out his hands so his dad could remove the post breakfast stickiness.

"I don't know."

"But I want to," Austin said, his lower lip beginning to quiver.

Tom knew how tired they all were after the previous day's "family presentations" and the Lockhart party for Emma in the evening. He also knew his sons were capable of powering through.

"I know you do, buddy." Tom hugged his son, then went around to minister to Bowie. "But Emma's really, really busy today so we might just have to work on our secret surprise for her. You know?"

"Right," Bowie said.

Austin breathed a sigh of relief, as Tom washed his face and hands. "We almost told her!"

"But we didn't," Crockett claimed.

Only because Emma was too distracted to put two and two together, Tom thought.

Aware they had already missed the first bell, he unlatched his son's belts, one after another, and handed them their backpacks. "Ready to go?"

They nodded in unison, already looking weary and their day hadn't even started yet.

It would be an early bedtime for them tonight, Tom mused. And maybe then he and Emma could really talk.

Until then, he had work to do, he thought, as he headed for the post office.

Emma had just gotten out of the shower and pulled on a robe when the buzzer sounded. Hoping it wasn't a family member, popping in to fish for more information, she pressed the intercom and said, "Yes?"

"It's Tom." His low, masculine voice sent tingles down her spine. "The kitchen faucet finally came in. Okay if I come in and do the repair?"

Her feelings were in such a jumble, she wanted to say no. But she also knew if she had let him do something to fix it in the first place, she wouldn't have gotten drenched just minutes before her meeting with the RTW Bridal exec.

It was never good to put off until tomorrow what could be done today.

"Sure." She was going to be working down in the studio anyway. "I'll unlock the door. Just let yourself in. I'm getting dressed."

He was waiting for her when she walked out of the bedroom. He hadn't had time to shave that morning before they left the ranch, and the rim of beard gave him a ruggedly sexy aura.

His glance drifted over her button-up white shirt and faded jeans. The shearling lined moccasins on her feet. She had blow-dried her hair and twisted it in a clip on the back of her head. She could almost feel him itching to take it down.

Not sure they should go there, after what had happened the evening before, she turned her attention to the new chrome faucet he had unwrapped. Made in the same style as the one he was replacing, it shone in the morning sunlight. "Well," she said, "I'll leave you to it…"

He caught her hand as she passed. Reeled her back in to his side.

"Not," he said with a commanding glance, "before we finally talk."

Tom felt Emma tense.

Not about to let her run away again, he kept his hold on her hand and led her over to the sofa. "You're still angry with me about the surprise party."

She sighed and shook her head, candidly meeting his eyes. "You should have given me a heads-up!"

He sat down beside her, his jean-clad knee bumping her denim-covered thigh. "I couldn't."

Anger glittered in her pretty eyes. She glared at him, the barriers around her heart firmly back in place. He told himself that was okay. He had coaxed her to open herself back up to a rekindled romance with him once; he could do it again.

"Obviously—" she jerked her hand free "—I do not see it that way."

"There wasn't much time to think about it, Emma. Susannah called me yesterday and told me she was taking Buttercup to the Circle L, so you'd have to pick her up there. Your mom thought you would probably want me and the boys there, to help celebrate the opening of your new design studio."

She raked her teeth across her lower lip. "That's really how it was presented to you?"

He nodded. "As just a surprise party celebrating all your hard work. I had no idea they knew that you were meeting with Barbara Roswald, or would be cracking open the champagne prematurely."

Her slender shoulders slumped. She let out a rough exhalation of breath. "So I'm not wrong to be ticked off about that…"

He reached over and gave her hand a brief squeeze. "They all meant well."

Emma looked down at their entwined fingers. Unhappiness tautened the delicate lines of her face. "Yes, well… All they did was put more pressure on me to seal a deal." Her voice took on a troubled note. "And you and I both know that might not happen."

Happy she hadn't pulled away from his attempt to comfort her, he tucked an errant strand of hair behind her ears. "It also might," he told her optimistically.

She frowned. And went silent once again. Wordlessly, she went to the window and stood there, with her hands in her back pockets, gazing out at the activity on the town streets. In that moment, she looked as lonely and alone as he had felt after their breakup, years ago.

"Did anything else happen during the meeting yesterday? That you haven't told me about?"

Not that she had revealed much.

He joined her at the window. Faced her, one shoulder braced against the frame. "Anything that made you feel conflicted?" he pressed.

Bingo.

She pivoted partway toward him. "Not exactly."

He waited, hoping she would trust him enough to confide in him. Finally, she did. "When Barbara Roswald was getting ready to leave, she mentioned that they have stores in all fifty states. Which I already knew. Then she asked me if I would be open to traveling to all their locations, should we strike a deal, to personally sell the wedding boot."

Tom forced himself to keep his tone casual. "Sounds reasonable," he remarked.

Emma drew a deep breath. She gazed at him, looking more inherently gorgeous than ever. "She also asked me if I would be amenable to moving to Chicago and working at headquarters."

Moving to Chicago. Tom took a moment to absorb that possibility. Knowing she needed him to be supportive no matter what, in the way he had not been in the past, he quashed his own feelings. Then asked gently, "And you said...?"

Now she really looked sad and conflicted. "Yes."

He understood she had been put on the spot. "And now you're regretting having agreed so readily," he guessed.

"I'm aware relocating there may come with the territory. But…" Her phone rang.

She looked at the screen. "That's Barbara Roswald's assistant." She put the phone to her ear and walked away. "Hi, Mimi," she said, her tone brisk and cheerful. "What's up? Mmm-hmm. I should probably be writing this down. Oh, okay. Thank you. Yes. We'll talk then."

She tapped the red button on the screen and ended the call. "They've set up Zoom interviews with the entire RTW Bridal team tomorrow, from nine to one."

"That was fast."

She wrinkled her nose. "Barbara said, before she left, that if they decided to move on this, they would move quickly. She wasn't kidding." She lifted a staying hand. "Not that I have a deal yet, or even a promise of one."

But she would. He knew that as suddenly as he was standing here watching her get ready to once again walk away from him, and everything she loved about being in Laramie, Texas, for the sake of her ambition.

Back then, he'd thought their love could and would easily be replaced.

Now he knew better.

Trying to put his own gnawing worries aside, he asked quietly, "Do you need any help with anything?"

She let out a shaky laugh and ran a hand through her hair, seeming to forget for a moment she had put it up in a clip. Her eyes lasered in on his. "How are you at settling a really bad case of nerves?"

Chapter Eighteen

Emma regretted the impulsive words the second they were out. This was not the time to be hitting on Tom when he was likely getting ready to walk away from whatever this was they'd had the last two weeks, just like he had before.

He apparently didn't see it that way.

"Well, as it happens, Princess Lady Emma—" he tipped an imaginary hat at her, before closing the distance and taking her in his arms "—I am actually *very good* at helping my woman relax."

My woman.

Had he just called her that?

She had no time to ponder. His head was slanting, his lips fastened on hers, and just that quickly the world seemed to stop spinning out of control, and she was brought back to the here and now. Basking in the wonder of being in his arms. Sheltered. Protected. And adored.

He took the clip out of her hair and combed his fingers through her hair. He gazed down at her lovingly. "I've got time, if you've got time," he said.

Emma knew, even if she hadn't, she would have made the time to make love with him again. To be one before everything got really crazy...

"That I do," she whispered, taking him by the hand and leading him toward her bedroom. Wise or not, she wanted to lose herself in the bliss, the intimacy, only he could bring. She hitched in a breath as his hands slid beneath the hem of her shirt and moved higher. He unfastened her bra and ran his thumbs across the tender crests, causing her to lose herself in him again.

She hadn't allowed herself to want anything but work for a long time. Hadn't allowed herself to hope they could have anything this close to a fairy tale.

The joy inside her bubbling up, she returned his kiss with everything she had. Surrendering against him. Letting him take total control.

They dropped down on the bed, and she arched against him. The yearning swirling through her escalated into an incessant ache. And still it wasn't enough. Swiftly, they helped each other undress. Naked, they came together again. She ran her hands over his hard muscles and smooth skin. His sculpted pecs and abs were absolutely divine. And lower still...

He wanted her. Fiercely. Uninhibitedly. Just as she wanted him.

They rolled onto their sides, so they were facing each other. And still they kissed and touched, and loved and stroked, until their bodies were filled with searing heat.

Her whole body throbbed as he slid a hand between her legs, making her blossom, sending her quickly to the brink.

She found him, too, loving and adoring until he too could stand it no more.

Together, they located a condom, rolled it on. He stretched out over top of her. She arched to receive him. Guided him inside her. Sensations ran riot inside her. She felt connected to him, heart and soul. Sweet moments passed. Tension built. And then they were blissful, flying, free. Catapulted into oblivion. Holding and keeping each other close. Until there was nothing but this sizzling hot connection. Nothing but each other and this moment in time…

"Daddy, how come Buttercup is with you?" Crockett asked Tom when he picked the boys up at school, later that afternoon.

"Yeah. Where is Princess Lady Emma?" Bowie tossed his backpack on the floor of the quad cab.

"I want to see her," Austin said.

Tom helped his sons up into the passenger compartment, one after another. He tried not to wonder if this, rather than the nights they had spent together the last two weeks, was really the harbinger of evenings to come. Deliberately, he pushed his own loneliness aside and said, "She's working, guys. So, I told her we would take care of Buttercup for her tonight and tomorrow, until she gets all her stuff done." He stowed their backpacks on the floor of the cab, against the front seats, making an aisleway for them to walk through. "You'll help me, won't you?"

"Sure," the boys chimed in unison, lining up in front of their seats.

"Is Princess Lady Emma coming for dinner?" Bowie asked hopefully.

Tom gave Buttercup, who was watching from the front seat, a pat on her silky head. She, too, seemed to wonder where her mistress was. "Not tonight," he said.

"Will she come by after and sleep over then?" Crockett climbed into his safety seat and put the harness over his shoulders.

Another wave of disappointment poured through him. "Afraid not," Tom said.

"How about breakfast tomorrow, then?" Austin asked, snapping the buckle closure on his harness.

Tom realized how dependent his sons had grown on Emma. Trying not to think how they would react if she got the deal she was seeking and moved to Chicago, never mind how crestfallen he would privately feel, he admitted as matter-of-factly as he could, "She'll be working then, too."

"But we want to see her!" Austin cried, looking on the verge of tears.

"Me, too, buddy." Tom hugged his son. "But sometimes grown-ups have to work long hours. You know that."

All three boys paused to consider what he'd said.

"Like when you're moving cattle on the ranch?" Crockett asked.

Tom climbed behind the wheel. "Exactly."

The triplets were silent as he drove out of town, toward his ranch. Buttercup curled up on the leather bench seat beside him and put her head on his thigh. Acting as if she too needed comfort. Fortunately, he was able to remind them, "Don't forget. Grandma will be coming home in *two* days. Today is Thursday, tomorrow is Friday and Grandma comes back on Saturday."

"Will Princess Lady Emma sleep over after Gramma comes home?" Bowie asked.

Good question. Especially because then he would have another family member to watch the kids, and he could drive Emma home himself.

Should she still be in Laramie, anyway.

He had the unsettling feeling that was not going to be the case.

At least not often.

Aware from the silence the boys were still waiting for his reply, he caught their glances in the rearview mirror. And said, as honestly as he could, "Probably not unless the weather is bad or something like that."

"But we *will* see her, right?" Austin said.

Tom sure hoped so.

His boys' hearts would be broken if she left their lives as abruptly as she had entered them.

As would his.

Which meant he would have to do everything possible to make sure she and Buttercup remained a part of his and the boys' "family," even if the future didn't look exactly like any of them had originally envisioned.

"Are there any other questions I can answer for you?" Emma asked early the following day as the four hour virtual interview came to an end.

Barbara Roswald exchanged glances with her team. All shook their heads.

Which was no surprise.

Each and every one of the executives had been very thorough.

Barbara turned back to Emma. She smiled. "Then we're ready to make our offer. Here it is…"

Emma listened.

Although she didn't absorb all that much after the first figures were announced.

"Mimi is emailing you the offer sheet now," Barbara said several minutes later.

Emma pulled herself together, responding like the businesswoman she was at heart. "I'm going to have to have my attorney look over it," she told her.

"Of course. Feel free to take the weekend. We want an answer by Monday, though. Because although you're our first choice," Barbara said, "and we really would love to have you and your wedding boot carrying our brand name, we really need to get moving on this ASAP…"

They had already alluded to the fact they were actively considering another designer, who had created a spectacular wedding sandal, if they failed to reach an agreement with her. Emma didn't doubt they would sign her rival, if she weren't as amenable as they wished to their terms.

Talk about playing hardball, she thought. Was this what it felt like to play in the big leagues? "Right."

The team signed off. Barbara said goodbye. And then the screen went blank.

Exhausted, Emma closed her laptop computer and got up from the worktable, where she had taken the meeting, and walked up to the sanctity of her apartment on wobbly legs. A text came in.

Hope all is going well, Tom wrote. Let me know if you want me to drop Buttercup off.

It would be helpful to have her dog with her. She had missed her the previous night, more than she could have imagined. Tom and the boys, too. Which just showed her how much her life had changed the past two weeks. And how much it could change in the next two, as well.

Anytime is good, Emma texted back, anxious to see him again. Although it had only been twenty-four hours or so since they had seen each other, it felt like much more. Meetings are done for the day.

Be there in twenty, he messaged in return.

Which likely meant he was at the ranch.

Aware she had time to make a cup of tea, Emma went to the kitchen sink and turned on the gleaming new faucet that Tom had installed for her. She filled the electric teakettle, added two bags to two cups, got the leftover tea cakes and sandwiches out of the fridge and then sat down to wait.

Tom arrived, Buttercup in tow. He was clean-shaven and freshly showered, wearing a dark green button-up shirt, jeans and boots. He smelled good, too. Like soap and sun and man.

Buttercup dashed across the floor, her tail wagging ferociously, and leaped up onto Emma's lap, licking her beneath the chin.

She laughed and snuggled her dog close.

Tom ambled closer. Whatever he felt about all that was going on, the changes that could happen next, was indecipherable. The corners of his sensual lips curved up. "She missed you," he said huskily. "We all did."

Emma patted the sofa cushion, inviting him to sit, too. Their gazes locked. "I missed you-all as well," she admitted, just as softly.

She had missed having Tom to talk with. Missed the boys and the growing sense of family they enjoyed. And she had especially missed feeling like she and Tom were a team when dealing with his outrageously funny and energetic little boys.

His gaze drifted over her, taking in her sophisticated black business dress. "So…?"

Trying not to get caught up in how big and strong and masculine he looked, she said, "You were right. They made an offer."

Approval radiated in his gaze. "Was it a good one?"

Her feelings surprisingly mixed, she inclined her head to one side. "It starts with a seven figure signing bonus."

For a moment he didn't move or even breathe.

Which was pretty much the reaction she'd had. "That's fantastic."

It was. And it wasn't.

Their eyes locked. Emotion vibrated between them.

He exhaled, his expression turning even more serious. "What else?"

Emma drew a deep breath. Nervous about what she was about to tell him next. "An immediate start. They would want me in Chicago next week and would set me up with an apartment locator, to help me quickly find a place. Additionally, they will pay all my moving expenses, and travel, when I eventually hit the road to publicize the addition of the wedding boot to all their stores."

Arms folded, Tom observed, "Sounds like the company is going all-out."

They were. And yet…for a lot of reasons, she wasn't completely sold on the opportunity to go into business with RTW Bridal. Not at all.

Tom, however, looked as if he thought it was all a done deal. One he had expected and was okay with. She tried not to think what it might mean, that he would be so willing to let her leave…for her career… again…

"Sounds like a once-in-a-lifetime opportunity," he said, giving her a long look.

It was. It completely validated all the time and energy she had put into her designs. All the sacrifices she had made…

It did not, however, honor everything else she wanted out of life.

Like Tom.

His kids.

Even Buttercup would have to sacrifice greatly in this new arrangement.

If she took it, that was.

Oblivious to her thoughts, Tom wrapped her in a big bear hug. "I'm so proud of you," he rasped, before letting her go and stepping back.

Emma took the time to drink him in. Where was his ambivalence? Shouldn't the fact that if she said yes, that she would have to leave Texas in a few days, have conjured up even a smidge of sorrow on his part? Yet he was still beaming at her. Happy. Encouraging. Like this was the best deal ever. Even for him. "You have earned every bit of this," he told her.

They were standing so close she could feel the heat emanating from his powerful body. She found herself wanting to kiss him again. Do more than that, actually. "Thank you."

He was distracted, too. His gaze roved over her features before returning to her eyes. He cupped her shoulders between his palms, then paused to look down at her, taking the time to drink her in. "I want you to know I support you one thousand percent."

That was good. *Wasn't it*?

"That I understand you are going to want to put your career first."

Irritated he still hadn't said one word about how much he was going to miss her if she took this gig, when that was all that she could think about, she frowned.

He looked her in the eye, promising in a gruff sexy voice that stirred her senses, "I'll do everything I can to make that possible."

Meaning what? she wondered. Was he planning to visit her? Bring the boys? Watch Buttercup for her when she had to hit the road, maybe for days and weeks at a time?

"So, you don't have to worry about the design studio here, or the apartment," he told her matter-of-factly. "You can keep the space. Or give it up whenever it is convenient. There will be no issues with the timing or the lease. Whatever makes your life easier is all right with me."

Emma was so disappointed in him she could barely speak. A smile pasted on her face, she said, "That's really generous of you."

Tom let go of her, stepped back. He braced his hands on his waist. The way he did before he started any important project. "I wasn't very supportive of you the last time around." He sized her up the same way he sized up a task. "I'm not going to make the same mistake twice."

And apparently, she thought sadly, surprised and shocked she had read him all wrong, again, *you're not going to fall for me, the way I've already fallen for you...again...*

Because if he had, none of this would be so easy for him. He wouldn't be so ready to let her go off to conquer the fashion world, with a smile and a wave goodbye...

"I just have one request." He paused deliberately,

drew a breath, then went on, even more soberly. "The boys all adore you and have come to really depend on you. So, whatever we can do to facilitate this transition for them, make your absence from their daily lives easier, I would appreciate." He frowned. "Even if it is just Zoom calls and emails, whatever…"

She understood him wanting to protect his children. What she didn't understand was why he wouldn't want anything for himself. Weekend visits. A long distance love arrangement. *Something.* The fact he wasn't asking for that, could only mean one thing.

Her cynicism increased, forcing her to conclude, "So, you are breaking up with me."

"Breaking up?" he repeated, his expression maddeningly inscrutable. He stared at her for a long moment, finally expressing the anger and frustration she had expected all along. It melded with her own. "First of all," he returned succinctly, "it hasn't been clear to me that you thought we were ever officially a couple again…"

He was right. There had been no official dating. No promise of exclusivity…

And yet when they had been alone together, it had felt as if they were not just picking up where they had left off, but forging new bonds of closeness and permanence. Had she misread everything? "The lovemaking…?"

He exhaled, clearly exasperated and ambivalent. Just as she was. "You were pretty clear that was just sex between friends and former lovers, remember? A temporary arrangement that might or might not lead to other things, depending on whether you decided to stay in Texas, or chase your dreams elsewhere."

Except it had started to feel like so much more than that to her! She had thought…hoped…he was feeling the same way.

But, like the logical businessman he was, the verbal contract they had forged at the outset was what he focused on. On the promises they had actually made. Instead of their private wishes and dreams.

He shook his head at her. "That *was* our deal, right? To take it day by day for a couple of weeks while my mom was gone. To not put any undue pressure or expectations on each other, the way we did before. And especially not anything that would interfere with your career ambitions."

Except it felt like he had gone from having one foot out the door, to having both feet out the door. It felt like he saw what challenges could be ahead and was trying to walk away, before things got difficult or messy.

"I'm trying to honor that, Emma," he continued gruffly.

Honor it or protect his heart? The same way she was suddenly moving to guard hers. Abruptly feeling near tears, she lifted her hand.

"While simultaneously and successfully pushing me out of your life," she said in a low, strangled voice.

So they wouldn't have to have an emotionally wrenching end to their romance all over again!

His eyes darkened with resentment. He exhaled roughly, looking as ticked off as she felt. He folded his arms across his chest. "What are you talking about?"

Their mutual fear of failure. Especially when it came to their relationship. She raked her hands through her hair, reluctantly accepting that maybe this was *all* preordained. "Travis warned me this would happen. That things between us would cool again when you no longer needed my help with the triplets during Marjorie's absence."

She shook her head in misery.

He sobered, confirming her worst suspicions.

"It just so happened to coincide with my big offer from RTW Bridal, which makes it all the more convenient for you."

Tom's features tightened with anger. For a second, his face bore the look of a warrior about to head into battle. "If anyone is looking for a way out, Emma," he told her tersely, "it seems to be you."

Ignoring the ache in her heart, she forced herself to do the right thing and let him go. "Tell me that you're not the slightest bit relieved that I did get an offer that will likely take me out of state again. I mean, you're obviously happy about the fact we won't be able to see each other much, if at all, if I do take it..."

When just the thought of being away from him that much made her feel sick and miserable.

Like none of it was going to be worth it. No matter how much money and success they threw at her. Yet he was steadfastly upbeat about the future that would have them living and working thousands of miles apart.

Tom stared her down. The unprecedented awkwardness between them increased. "You really think that little of me after everything I've done to help you succeed the past two weeks?" he asked bitterly.

They'd been trading favor for favor. One friend and former lover to another. No matter how she had tried to romanticize it, sadly, it had never been more than mutually doled out assistance. And some superhot sex.

"I think the boys are right. We have been living in a fairy tale." Emma grimaced, as angry at herself for her foolishness, as she was at him. "Only there is no glass slipper to ultimately bring us back together." No way to make him want her and love her the way she needed... Her spine stiff, she walked over to show him the door. Ready finally for the hurting each other to be over, once and for all. "And there never will be."

Chapter Nineteen

"Are you planning to tell me what is going on?" Marjorie asked Tom early the next evening, after he had gotten the triplets to bed. "Or are you just going to leave it to me to guess?"

And just like that, the mom who had nosed her way into his affairs his entire life was back. Grimacing, he slid the dinner dishes into the dishwasher. "What do you mean?"

His mom wiped down the counters and cleared the table. "The boys have not stopped talking about Princess Lady Emma and her adorable dog Buttercup. You, on the other hand, have said *nothing*."

Because it hurt to even think about how high his hopes had been, only to have them crushed yet again. He shrugged, avoiding her probing look. "That's because the boys were doing all the talking." He broke down the takeout pizza boxes and put them in the trash.

Finished cleaning, his mom closed the distance between them and touched his arm gently. "Well, they're asleep now. And it's just you and me. So, honey. *What happened?*"

Tom figured he probably should tell her. She would hear about it soon enough anyway when Emma announced her big news. "Emma got a big offer from a company that owns 225 bridal shops across the entire country."

Seven figures.

How could he compete with that?

He walked over to brew himself a cup of regular coffee while his mother set about making herself a latte from her fancy espresso machine. "They want her to move to Chicago next week." He turned to face his mom. Holding up a palm before she could interrupt. "And no, I haven't told the boys yet. I don't even know if she has announced it to her family since she doesn't formally have to respond to the company until Monday."

Marjorie nodded, thinking. The aroma of fresh brewed coffee filled the room. "So, there is still time to change her mind."

As much as he wanted to keep her close, he could not rob her of the success she deserved. He regarded his mom patiently. "Mom, this is the opportunity Emma has always wanted. The big career she always thought she would have."

Marjorie stirred vanilla syrup into her drink, then motioned for him to have a seat at the kitchen table, opposite her. "I may be reading too much into the situation, but I have a feeling—from what I saw during my video chats with you-all while I was in Italy—that the last two weeks with you and the boys have shown her that she wants a lot more than just work out of life."

Tom had thought so, too. But if that had been the truth, then wouldn't she have been a lot more conflicted about the relocation requirement of the job she was being offered?

Instead, she had repeated the information about the need to move to Chicago right away, matter-of-factly. Like it was something she could deal with, in order to get what she ultimately wanted. Fame and money. Indisputable proof of her talent as a designer.

He cupped his mug in front of him. Feeling more ambivalent than he ever remembered being in his life.

Marjorie went on kindly, "I think being with the boys so much has helped her realize she wants kids, too. And to be back together with you…"

He *wished*. Heart clenching in his chest, Tom shook his head. The pain inside him escalated. "Then you're wrong," he said. Too restless to sit a second longer, he got up.

His mother rose, too, and began to get out the ingredients for the boys' favorite peanut butter cookies. She put the stick of butter into the microwave to soften. "Did you give Emma another choice?"

Tom paced the kitchen, mug of coffee in hand, feeling as restless as a trapped mountain lion. He stared out at the descending dusk. "Like...?" he commanded gruffly.

Marjorie put brown sugar into the mixing bowl.

"The promise of a real future with you and the boys," she huffed. "And not just some half measure with you in the background, while she goes off to become a famous and wealthy shoe designer."

Like his boys, sometimes his mother was way too romantic. He set his mug down with a thud. "Mom, the last thing she wanted from me yesterday was an impulsive proposal of marriage."

"I agree. That simply wouldn't cut it. But, on the other hand, if you were to approach her seriously..."

Tom stared at his mother in exasperation. She was making this all sound simple. It wasn't. "What are you saying?" he demanded.

"That it's possible," Marjorie returned carefully, "that after first losing Emma, then Vicki, that maybe deep down you're afraid to put everything on the line again?"

Tom wished that weren't true. But in his heart, he knew it was. Suffering another loss even more daunting than the first two he had suffered might bring him to his knees. He wasn't sure he could afford that, not if he wanted to be the kind of strong, resolute dad his boys needed.

"This will be the third time I've let the woman in my life down, Mom."

"So you screwed up with Emma. Again. It's still not too late," his mom decreed quietly. She looked him in the eye. "It's *never* too late to open up your heart and make amends."

* * *

Ten miles away, Emma sat at the kitchen table with her parents. She had excluded them earlier, so she wanted to break the news about the offer she had received to them first. They listened intently, as she ran down all the pluses and minuses of the deal being presented to her by RTW Bridal.

They were as proud as she had expected them to be. And as encouraging as always when it came to her pursuing her dreams.

"Well, first of all," her dad said, like the businessman-rancher he was, "you can let your attorney work on the things you aren't happy about."

Emma gestured at all the items on the official offer sheet she had asterisked as problematic for her. "They aren't going to budge on any of the big items, Dad. They were already clear about that."

Her mom frowned. "So, they're pressuring you."

She shrugged. Yes, they were, but that wasn't what hurt the most. It was Tom's reaction. Or more accurately, *nonreaction* to her big news that was bothering her. And leaving her feeling like she had just had her heart broken, all over again.

Robert took Carol's hand. As always her parents were one in their love for each other, and for her. "We can certainly see why you are so conflicted," he observed.

"It doesn't sound like moving to Chicago is what you want," her mom said carefully.

She was right. Emma didn't want to be that far from her family ever again. And yet... She looked her parents in the eye, really needing their advice. "The thing is, I probably won't ever get another offer like this one."

Her parents exchanged looks. "Money isn't everything," her dad reminded her.

And Emma knew he meant it.

"True, but are people going to think I'm a fool if I walk away from what is, in a whole lot of respects, a dream come true?"

"If the offer from RTW Bridal was the only consideration and making lots of money was your ultimate goal, then yes, it would be shortsighted and you would definitely regret it," her mom said, getting up to pour everyone more coffee. "But if you want more out of life than just work, you need to think about that, too, about where you are likely to find the love and intimate personal connections that you need to be happy."

Relief flowed through Emma. So her folks *did* understand her conundrum! More so than she had expected them to. She felt her lower lip tremble slightly. "But what if what I want is not what Tom wants?"

Her dad squinted. "Have you asked him?"

Emma's heart sank. This was the one thing in her life, the only thing really, that she was afraid to face head-on. "No," she admitted in a low, miserable sounding tone.

"Why not?" her mom asked.

Emma gestured helplessly, suddenly feeling near tears for the twentieth time that weekend. "Because…" Her parents waited patiently as she swallowed around the growing knot of emotion in her throat. "I was afraid of what he'd say if I told him how conflicted I was. Afraid he would want to stick to his plan to never marry again and put me in the just-really-good-friends category forever." Her heart ached as she finished.

"I suppose that could happen," her mom conceded honestly.

Although Carol didn't look as if she thought it would, Emma noted hopefully.

"But, darlin', in the end," her dad added seriously, "in order to really find peace, in both your work and in your personal life, you have to follow your heart. Even if it means putting your pride on the line, too."

Emma returned to her apartment with Buttercup, knowing what she had to do. She had just finished sending the letter to Barbara Roswald when the buzzer sounded. It was Tom. "Can we talk?" he asked in the low husky voice she loved.

A shiver of anticipation went through her. She drew a deep, bolstering breath. "Come on up."

A minute later, he was at her door, as strong and steady and invincible as he had always been. And yet as raw and vulnerable, too.

It had only been a little more than twenty-four hours since they had seen each other, but it felt like forever, as she ushered him inside her apartment. His hair was tousled, as if he had been running his hands through it all evening, but his handsome face was devoid of the usual evening scruff. Which meant he had shaved before coming over.

She caught a whiff of his masculine cologne and

the mint of his toothpaste as he neared. A black Henley stretched across his broad shoulders, nicely delineating the sexy musculature of his chest and abs. Dark jeans and brown boots did equally nice things to his lower half.

As he turned to her, his expression was solemn, but inscrutable. Hoping he wanted what she did out of their relationship, she felt her heart kick against her ribs. "Your mom get back from Italy okay?"

As they squared off, his gaze took in her cap-sleeved yellow tee and white denim skirt. She worried that she didn't look as put together as she had at the beginning of what had been a very long day, but the appreciative gleam in his eyes said he found her every bit as delectable as she found him. "Oh yeah." The crinkles around the corners of his eyes deepened. "She slept the entire way back from Italy, so she is brimming with energy. She's at the ranch, baking cookies as we speak."

Emma watched Buttercup dash over to see Tom. He hunkered down to pet her affectionately. "The Alphabet Gang must have been glad to see her."

He stood. Towering over her once again. "They were," he drawled, a familiar twinkle in his eyes. "But they've been missing you, too."

Fear moved past the excitement roaring through her. She knew she couldn't bear it if they disappointed each other again. She regarded him steadily, her guard up. "I'm sorry about that."

He came closer still, his eyes leveled on hers. "Me, too," he said softly. "I haven't handled things as well as I wanted." His voice dropped to a sexy rumble, his gaze devouring her from head to toe.

Her heart pounded all the harder. Now was the time. To sacrifice her pride, and open up her heart, and hope he would fully open up his in return. "Me, neither." She took his hands in hers and tilted her face up to his. Drawing a bolstering breath, she said, "Which is why I need to tell you about the offer from RTW Bridal."

The tips of his fingers caressed the back of her hands, eliciting tingles. "And I'd like to hear it. But first," he continued ruefully, as he drew her over to sit on the sofa beside him, "I need to say this." Still holding on to her palms, he turned to face her, his eyes full of things she was almost afraid to read.

Gruffly, he continued, "Yesterday, I told you what I thought you wanted and needed to hear from me. That unlike before—" regret flashed on his handsome face "—when I was more concerned about my own needs than yours, that I support you and your ambition one thousand percent." His gaze narrowed. "Meaning, although this is the part in retrospect that may not have been clear to you, that I would always be here for you, however you needed me. Even if it meant that for the next two years we had to live in different states."

Emma hitched in a breath, suddenly afraid where this might be going. To another, albeit gentler, breakup. "And I appreciate that," she told him, surprised she could sound so composed when she was on the verge of falling apart on the inside. Again.

His regard grew more intense. "But I didn't tell you

the most important part," he said, his voice firm and strong. "Which is that I love you, Emma."

She fought back a grin.

He threaded his hands through her hair, then continued, "I have always loved you, from the time we were kids. Through all the years we dated." He jerked in a rough breath. "Even when we broke up, and we thought we had both moved on, and made other lives for ourselves, the part of me that loved you was just on Pause. Still there. But buried deep inside."

It had been that way for her, too, Emma thought, as joy took flight inside her.

He stood and took her into his arms. His body was warm and strong against hers. "It wasn't until we started spending time together again that I realized that as committed as I was to Vicki, and the life we shared, I know now that I've never loved anyone the way I love you." He gazed down at her, repentant and somber. "And I never will."

She splayed her hands over the steady thrumming of his heart. She hitched in a breath. "Oh, Tom. I love you, too. So much!"

He slanted his head over hers and delivered a sizzling kiss. Emma was trembling with desire when he finally broke off the kiss and lifted his head. He grinned, sharing the quiet satisfaction and hope she felt. "Maybe this is what we should have led with yesterday?" he teased.

"We might have had a better ending to that conversation," Emma agreed shakily, forcing herself to reveal her issues, as well. "Or...not," she admitted honestly.

Her voice caught and she leaned in. "Because I have been hiding my feelings, too."

His irises darkened as he listened.

"When I said it was okay with me that you had ruled out marriage for your future. That we were just going to be friends, our love affair temporary—" her voice caught "—it was never what I really wanted."

He looked surprised. Then relieved. "Then why…?" he asked gently.

Emma shrugged, knowing he would understand, if she told him all of it. "I was hedging my bets." She blinked back the tears that threatened. "Trying to protect us from having another wrenching breakup."

Soberly, he said, "We almost had one yesterday anyway."

"*Almost* being the important word." She hugged him again, savoring his heat and his strength.

He stroked a hand through her hair. "So you and I are good?"

"Yes." Satisfaction roared through her. "Although we still have a lot to discuss." A lot he had to know. She extricated herself from his arms. "I want you to see the offer that was presented to me, so you will know why I have decided to turn it down."

She went and got him the offer sheet.

Waited while he read through it.

"Wow, this is one-sided."

"I know. Right? Their noncompete clause means I would be unable to design or sell any of my own shoes any longer."

"Plus RTW Bridal would own all your intellectual

property. And be able to license and produce it or not, as they saw fit."

"And they weren't going to budge on that. And that was depressing as all get out to me, Tom. I've really missed not being able to work in my studio the past few weeks. Plus I really wanted to explore making pretty, comfortable, easy-to-wear shoes that can handle all kinds of orthotic inserts, for older women. That is an untapped market, at least around here." She drew a deep breath, needing him to understand and support her on this, too. "Which is why I wrote to Barbara Roswald and thanked her and her team for their time and consideration and rejected their offer."

Tom was as supportive as she had hoped he would be. "Are you going to look for a new partner slash distributor?"

Emma shook her head. "No. This has taught me that I really like being my own boss and that money isn't the be-all and end-all for me. Having the support of the community and my family, and especially you and the boys, is. Plus the changes to my social media are also increasing interest in my studio. Which is why I am going to work like heck to make The Boot Lab the success I always envisioned it being."

He regarded her with all the respect she had ever wanted. "Good for you."

"So—" she spread her hands wide, beginning to feel like a princess in a fairy tale, despite all the challenges ahead of her "—that takes care of my professional life." And removed any business blockades between her and Tom.

"What about your personal life?"

And here it was, her biggest chance of all for happiness.

She'd told him how she felt about a no-strings affair versus something permanent and long-lasting. The question was, how did he feel? "That, cowboy," she said softly, "depends on you."

Here it was, Tom thought. The moment he had been waiting for. With none of the accoutrements he needed.

But, what the heck, those could come later.

He dropped down on one knee. Took her hands in his. And looked solemnly into her eyes. "Princess Lady Emma…"

She laughed, even as moisture sparkled in her eyes. She ruffled the tousled layers of his hair. "I can't believe you just said that."

He kissed the back of her hand, with breathtaking reverence. Then asked what he had wanted to, ever since she had come back into his life and filled it with love and laughter. "Would you do me the honor of becoming my wife?"

Shimmering with joy, she teased, "You're sure this is what you want?"

Her sweet sultry voice filling him with contentment, he rose and took her all the way into his arms. "Absolutely, incredibly, one million percent sure," he said, kissing her sweetly, deeply.

She wreathed her arms about his neck and kissed him back. "Well, what do you know, Wheeler-Dealer Cowboy Tom." She chuckled as he folded her even closer, so they were touching in one long electric line. The excited flush in her cheeks deepened, making her look all the more gorgeous. "Marrying you is what I want, too," she savored the sweet bliss of being in his arms. "So yes, of course I will marry you!"

They took the time to make love, then Tom drove Emma and Buttercup back out to the Rocking R ranch. They shared their news with Marjorie, who was absolutely delighted, and then, for the very first time, Emma spent the night in the guest room, instead of on the sofa.

The boys were ecstatic the next morning when they woke and found her.

There were hugs all around.

"Did you know it's Mother's Day?" they asked her.

Emma nodded. A lump grew in her throat as she guessed where this was headed. "Yep."

The triplets' excitement grew. "We gave Gramma her present yesterday when she got home from the airport, because we couldn't wait," Crockett announced importantly.

"And now we want to give you yours!" Bowie said.

Austin dashed out of the room. He came back with a messily wrapped box. "You gotta open it now. Right, Daddy?"

Tom was grinning from ear to ear.

Her heart filling, Emma drew a breath, protesting, "You know I'm not…yet…"

Tom shook his head, disagreeing. "In every way that counts you have been…" he said solemnly.

True, in her heart, she felt like these three sweet, sensitive and rambunctious boys were all hers.

"Okay." Marjorie appeared in the doorway, still clad in her robe, coffee cup in hand. "This, I have to see…" She was smiling, too.

"Hurry!" Austin jumped up and down.

"Yes! We can't wait!" Bowie clapped his hands.

"We know you're going to love it. Because it will get you what you really want," Crockett concluded.

Except I already have everything I really want, Emma thought, as she removed the ribbon and opened up the wrapping. Inside, was a shoebox that contained a pair of shoes just her size, from a store that specialized in Cinderella memorabilia.

"It's your glass slippers!" Austin shouted.

"And they have lights in them that makes them sparkle!" Bowie pointed out.

"Try 'em on so you can get your prince!" Crockett demanded.

Not about to disappoint her rowdy little darlings, after they had figured all this out, Emma swung her legs over the side of the bed and bent to put on a glass slipper. Tom knelt to assist. "Well, what do you know, it fits!" he said gruffly. His eyes filled at the significance of the moment.

So did Emma's.

"And now you can kiss and get married!" Crockett declared.

So Tom and Emma did.

Epilogue

The day before Mother's Day, one year later...

Tom snuggled with Emma on the love seat in the master bedroom. Together, they watched Buttercup stroll over to the full-length mirror and stand in front of it. The Australian labradoodle gazed at her reflection, tilting her head right, then left, before straightening once again. As she continued gazing at herself, her tail wagged happily.

Tom draped his arm over Emma's shoulders and brought her in close. She snuggled against him, even as he inclined his head affectionately at their family pet, inquiring, "Do you think the little pooch knows she's famous?"

Emma shifted, so she could see Tom's face. His skin

already bore a tan from the hours out in the spring sun. Her husband seemed to get more handsome every day. He had just had a shower and she inhaled the brisk masculine scent of his soap.

With effort, she returned her attention to his question about fame, in regard to their adorable curly haired golden labradoodle. "You mean, does Buttercup know that her likeness in the new logo for my business has become wildly popular, both online and around town? Technically, I don't see how she could. But I think she probably senses it...and she certainly feels the admiration of everyone who meets her..."

"No surprise there. She is pretty darn cute." Buttercup had been tapped to be The Boot Lab's mascot. Hence, a humorous painting of her proudly carrying the famous wedding boot adorned the design studio sign, as well as all the social media and packaging.

Emma turned and wrapped her arms about his neck. She moved in to give his lips a sweet and tender kiss. "You're cute, too."

Tom shifted her over onto his lap and kissed her back, just as reverently. "So are you, Mrs. Reid..."

She sighed, reveling in the endearment, as well as the next kiss.

From below, they could hear the sounds of the boys' excitement, rising to a fever pitch. Emma tamped down her desire, knowing they would have ample time and privacy to make love when the boys were asleep for the night.

More whoops and the sounds of something metal falling had even Buttercup turning her head to look.

Wondering exactly what was going on down there, Emma asked, "Think your mom needs some help supervising the triplet threat?"

Tom kissed the back of her hand and pointed to his phone screen, which was blank. "She wouldn't hesitate to let me know if she did, via text."

"True." All three adults in their household were very good at communicating.

Tom stroked a hand through Emma's hair. "Besides, it I were to go down there, I would ruin the surprise for us."

True. Emma smiled proudly. "The boys are really into gifting people things these days."

Tom reflected, "They like bringing joy to the family."

Emma snuggled closer. "I love being *part* of this family."

Tom slid his hand beneath her chin and lifted her face to his. His eyes sparkled with ardent lights. "No regrets, Princess Lady Emma?" he teased. "Even on our craziest, most challenging days?"

Emma shook her head. The occasional kindergarten drama was both gloriously challenging and immensely rewarding to her. She loved being there for The Alphabet Gang, shepherding them through the ups and downs of their lives. "Not a single one, Wheeler-Dealer Cowboy Tom..."

Seeing no reason to wait, after all the time they had wasted apart, they had married the previous June. Emma and Buttercup had moved into the Rocking R ranch with Tom, his mom and the three kids. By the time school had started, the boys were calling her "Mom." And she could barely recall a time when they were not a part of her life. Her days brimming with so much love and laughter.

And thanks to the targeted expansion of her customer base, and her new and improved social media, her business had grown by leaps and bounds.

She had hired two apprentices to help her make the footwear. Although she still crafted the more delicate shoes, too, her ever popular wedding boot was now available for order at independent bridal shops all over Texas. She no longer did trunk shows because she didn't want to be away from Tom and the kids on the weekends. Customers either worked with her online or came to her studio in Laramie instead.

Business and life were good. For her and for Tom.

As was their marriage...

Without warning, the three boys appeared in the open master bedroom doorway. All were wearing child-sized chef's aprons, smudged with whatever it was they had been preparing.

Crockett propped his hands on his hips. "Dinner's ready!"

"You're never going to guess what we helped Gramma make!" Bowie burst out excitedly.

"You're going to love it!" Austin predicted.

"I'm sure we will!" Emma and Tom walked downstairs with the boys. Buttercup followed.

The kitchen table had been set. Serving bowls and platters contained all the family favorites. Crispy golden Tater Tots, fluffy waffles, bacon and sausage, a big bowl of fresh strawberries and another of sliced peaches.

Emma pretended to be shocked. She turned to Tom.

"Breakfast for dinner!" she exclaimed with real pleasure.

Tom grinned and shook his head in awe. "Who would have thought?" he drawled.

"And we helped Gramma with everything!" Crockett boasted.

"Except we couldn't get near the stove or anything hot," Bowie cautioned.

"We have to be *safe*," Austin agreed.

"Well, it looks wonderful!" Emma said, as Tom held out her chair. She sat at one end of the table; he took the other. The kids and Marjorie were in between. They held hands and said grace. And then another lively family dinner began.

* * * * *

#2917 SUMMER NIGHTS WITH THE MAVERICK
Montana Mavericks: Brothers & Broncos • by Christine Rimmer
Ever since rancher Weston Abernathy rescued waitress Everlee Roberts at
Doug's Bar, he can't get her off his mind. But the spirited single mom has no interest
in a casual relationship, and Wes isn't seeking commitment. As the temperature
rises, Evy feels the heat, too, tempting her to throw her hat in the ring regardless of
what it might cost her heart...

#2918 A DOUBLE DOSE OF HAPPINESS
Furever Yours • by Teri Wilson
With three-year-old twins to raise, Ian Parson hires Rachel Gray hoping she'll solve
all their problems. And soon the nanny is working wonders with his girls...and Ian.
Rachel even has him agreeing to adopt a dog and cat because the twins love them.
He's laughing, smiling and falling in love again. But will Ian need a double dose of
courage to ask Rachel to stay...as his wife?

#2919 MATCHED BY MASALA
Once Upon a Wedding • by Mona Shroff
One impetuous kiss has turned up the heat on chef Amar Virani's feelings for
Divya Shah. He's been in love with her since high school, but a painful tragedy
keeps Amar from revealing his true emotions. While they work side by side in her
food truck, Divya is tempted to step outside her comfort zone and take a chance on
Amar—even if it means risking more than her heart.

#2920 THE RANCHER'S FULL HOUSE
Texas Cowboys & K-9s • by Sasha Summers
Buzz Lafferty's "no kids" policy is to protect his heart. But Jenna Morris sends
Buzz's pulse into overdrive. The beautiful teacher is raising her four young siblings...
and that's t-r-o-u-b-l-e. If only Jenna's fiery kisses didn't feel so darn right—and her
precocious siblings weren't so darn lovable. Maybe it's time for the Morris party of
five to become a Lafferty party of six...

#2921 WHAT TO EXPECT WHEN SHE'S EXPECTING
Sutter Creek, Montana • by Laurel Greer
Since childhood, firefighter Graydon Halloran has been secretly in love with
Alejandra Brooks Flores. Now, with Aleja working nearby, it's becoming impossible
for Gray to hide his feelings. But Aleja's situation is complicated. She's pregnant with
IUI twins and she isn't looking for love. Can Gray convince his lifelong crush that he
can make her dreams come true?

#2922 RIVALS AT LOVE CREEK
Seven Brides for Seven Brothers • by Michelle Lindo-Rice
When a cheating scandal rocks Shanna Jacobs's school, she's put under the
supervision of her ex, Lynx Harrington—who wants the same superintendent job.
Maybe their fledgling partnership will make the grade after all?

HSECNM0522

*Stationed in her hometown of Port Serenity, coast guard
captain Skylar Beaumont is determined to tough out
this less-than-ideal assignment until her transfer goes
through. Then she crashes into Dex Wakefield. She
hasn't spoken to her secret high school boyfriend in six
years—not since he broke her heart before graduation.
But when old feelings resurface, will the truth bring
them back together?*

Read on for a sneak peek at
Sweet Home Alaska,
the first book in USA TODAY bestselling author
Jennifer Snow's Wild Coast series.

Everything looked exactly the same as the day she'd left.

Though her pulse raced as she approached the marina and the
nondescript coast guard station, her heart swelled with pride at the
sight of the *Starlight* docked there. With its deep V, double chine
hull and all-aluminum construction, the forty-five-foot response
boat was designed for speed and stability in various weather
conditions. Twin diesel engines with waterjet propulsion eliminated
the need for propellers under the boat, making it safer in missions
where they needed to rescue a person overboard. Combined with
its self-righting capability to help with capsizing in rough seas, it
had greater speed and maneuverability than the older vessels. The
boat was the one thing she had total confidence in. And she would
be in charge of it and a crew of five.

The crew was the tougher part. She was determined to gain
their trust and respect. She was eager to show that she was one
of them but also maintain a professional distance. Her father and
grandfather made it look so easy, but she knew this would be her

hardest challenge, to command a crew of familiar faces. People she'd grown up with, people who remembered her as the little girl who'd wear her father's too-big captain hat as she sat in the captain's chair in the pilothouse.

Did that hat finally fit now?

Weaving the rental car along the winding road, and seeing the familiar Wakefield family yacht docked in the marina, her heart pounded. The fifty-footer had always been the most impressive boat in the marina, even now that it was over thirty years old. Its owner, Kurt Wakefield, had lived on the yacht for twenty-five years.

Kurt had died the year before. Skylar peered through the windshield to look at it. Had someone else bought the boat? Large bumpers had been added to the exterior, and pull lines could be seen on deck. She frowned. Had it been turned into some sort of rescue boat?

It wasn't unusual for civilians to aid in searches along the coast when requested, but the yacht was definitely an odd addition. There had never been a Wakefield who had shown interest in civil service to the community…except one.

The man standing on the upper deck now, pulling the lines. Wearing a pair of faded jeans and just a T-shirt, the muscles in his shoulders and back strained as he worked and Skylar's mouth went dry. She slowed the vehicle, unable to look away. Almost as if in slow motion, the man turned and their eyes met. Her breath caught as familiarity registered in his expression.

And unfortunately, the untimely unexpected sight of her ex-boyfriend—Dex Wakefield—had Skylar forgetting to hit the brakes as she reached the edge of the gravel lot next to the dock. Too late, her rental car drove straight off the edge and into the frigid North Pacific Ocean.

Don't miss
Sweet Home Alaska,
available May 2022 wherever
HQN books and ebooks are sold.

HQNBooks.com

PHJSEXP0522

Get 4 FREE REWARDS!

We'll send you 2 FREE Books plus 2 FREE Mystery Gifts.

FREE
Value Over
$20

Both the **Harlequin® Special Edition** and **Harlequin® Heartwarming™** series feature compelling novels filled with stories of love and strength where the bonds of friendship, family and community unite.

YES! Please send me 2 FREE novels from the Harlequin Special Edition or Harlequin Heartwarming series and my 2 FREE gifts (gifts are worth about $10 retail). After receiving them, if I don't wish to receive any more books, I can return the shipping statement marked "cancel." If I don't cancel, I will receive 6 brand-new Harlequin Special Edition books every month and be billed just $4.99 each in the U.S or $5.74 each in Canada, a savings of at least 17% off the cover price or 4 brand-new Harlequin Heartwarming Larger-Print books every month and be billed just $5.74 each in the U.S. or $6.24 each in Canada, a savings of at least 21% off the cover price. It's quite a bargain! Shipping and handling is just 50¢ per book in the U.S. and $1.25 per book in Canada.* I understand that accepting the 2 free books and gifts places me under no obligation to buy anything. I can always return a shipment and cancel at any time. The free books and gifts are mine to keep no matter what I decide.

Choose one: ☐ **Harlequin Special Edition**
(235/335 HDN GNMP)

☐ **Harlequin Heartwarming Larger-Print**
(161/361 HDN GNPZ)

Name (please print)

Address   Apt. #

City   State/Province   Zip/Postal Code

Email: Please check this box ☐ if you would like to receive newsletters and promotional emails from Harlequin Enterprises ULC and its affiliates. You can unsubscribe anytime.

Mail to the **Harlequin Reader Service:**
IN U.S.A.: P.O. Box 1341, Buffalo, NY 14240-8531
IN CANADA: P.O. Box 603, Fort Erie, Ontario L2A 5X3

Want to try 2 free books from another series! Call 1-800-873-8635 or visit www.ReaderService.com.

*Terms and prices subject to change without notice. Prices do not include sales taxes, which will be charged (if applicable) based on your state or country of residence. Canadian residents will be charged applicable taxes. Offer not valid in Quebec. This offer is limited to one order per household. Books received may not be as shown. Not valid for current subscribers to the Harlequin Special Edition or Harlequin Heartwarming series. All orders subject to approval. Credit or debit balances in a customer's account(s) may be offset by any other outstanding balance owed by or to the customer. Please allow 4 to 6 weeks for delivery. Offer available while quantities last.

Your Privacy—Your information is being collected by Harlequin Enterprises ULC, operating as Harlequin Reader Service. For a complete summary of the information we collect, how we use this information and to whom it is disclosed, please visit our privacy notice located at corporate.harlequin.com/privacy-notice. From time to time we may also exchange your personal information with reputable third parties. If you wish to opt out of this sharing of your personal information, please visit readerservice.com/consumerchoice or call 1-800-873-8635. **Notice to California Residents**—Under California law, you have specific rights to control and access your data. For more information on these rights and how to exercise them, visit corporate.harlequin.com/california-privacy.

HSEHW22

*When a cheating scandal rocks Shanna Jacobs's
school, she's put under the supervision of her ex,
Lynx Harrington—who wants the same superintendent
job she does. Maybe their fledgling partnership will
make the grade after all?*

Read on for a sneak peek at
Rivals at Love Creek,
*the first book in the brand-new
Seven Brides for Seven Brothers miniseries
and Michelle Lindo-Rice's debut with
Harlequin Special Edition!*

"Now, I know the circumstances aren't ideal, but I'm
looking forward to working with you."

She appeared to struggle, like she was thinking how
to formulate her words. "I wish I was working with you
by choice and not circumstance. Not that I would choose
to," she said with a chuckle.

"I hear you. If it weren't for this situation, we would
still be throwing daggers at each other during leadership
meetings."

"Put yourself in my shoes. If you were going through
this, how would you feel?" she asked, rubbing her toe
into the carpet. "Honest answer."

"I'm not as brave as you are, and I have more pride
than common sense."

She blushed and averted her eyes. "I would have resigned if I didn't have a mother and sister to consider. Pride is secondary to priority."

He felt ashamed and got to his feet. He went over to her. "You're right. I'm thinking like a single man. If I were married or had other responsibilities, I'd do what I'd have to and keep my job. I was hoping that Irene—" He stopped, unsure of the etiquette of bringing another woman into the conversation.

"No need to stop on my account. I know you had—have—a life."

Lynx wasn't about to talk about Irene, no matter how cool Shanna claimed she was with it. "I'm ready to fall in love, get married and install the white picket fence."

"How do you know you're ready?" she asked.

He rubbed his chin. "I'm at the brink of where I want to be professionally. I want someone to share my success with me."

"I get it," she said, doing that half-bite thing with her lip again.

Don't miss
Rivals at Love Creek
by Michelle Lindo-Rice,
available July 2022 wherever
Harlequin Special Edition books and ebooks are sold.

Harlequin.com